The Nation

By: Benjamin Bayani

This book is dedicated to my father Ben who never allowed me to give up on anything and my mother Teresa who was always there when I needed her no matter what. I love you both more than simple words on a page can describe.

Follow me on Facebook
http://www.facebook.com/TheNationBook

1

"Need tickets?" The scalper asked as Jack and Bobby emerged from Kenmore station. They just ignored him and kept walking. Ever since Bobby got pinched for buying tickets off of a scalper to one of the ever so popular Boston Fighting Cox and New York Minutemen baseball games, they stayed away. There was no need for them to get scalped tickets this time anyway.

It was a warm September night and Jack was feeling good. "There's something sacred about all of this, isn't there?" Jack was asking. "You know, like, the smell in the air or something. The feeling you get right before a big game."

"Oh yea, wait a second I definitely smell it," Bobby said sarcastically sniffing the air, "We went from smelling piss on the T to smelling motor exhaust in the air."

They were two cousins and the best of friends. Jack's father had been bringing them to Fighting Cox games for as long as they could remember. The Cox had been in a drought since 1918, but since winning the championship in '03, ticket sales for a Fighting Cox game went up and it was almost impossible to get tickets to a game, especially a Fighting Cox and Minutemen game, so they haven't been going to too many as of late. Jack worked for Callaghan

Tire, however, and they had lifetime season tickets that they gave out to their employees. This is the reason they had seats three rows up from the Fighting Cox dugout.

"You know what I mean, man!" Jack retorted as the vendors on Lansdowne St. were screaming at you to get your hot sausages.

"Yea I know I'm only fucking with you. Relax a little." Bobby replied as they neared the end of Lansdowne.

Jack paused a moment and looked at his cousin. Something had been weighing on his mind. He didn't want to bring it up, but it had to be said. He looked at Bobby with his most pleading eyes and said, "Just please don't drink too much. I do want to come back you know."

Bobby laughed, "You know me man, don't worry."

Jack shook his head and continued walking. "That's exactly what I mean. I know you and that's why I'm worried." They were rounding the corner and going onto Ipswich St.

"You seriously need to lighten up, brother. You ever wonder about that school, man?" Bobby asked pointing to the Boston Arts Academy/Fenway High School.

Jack gave him a weird look. "Dude, it's a fucking school, what is there to wonder?"

"I don't know, um, what is it for? Why does it say arts academy as well as high school? I don't know I just always wondered that's all." He replied defensively as they passed gate B and entered Van Ness St.

"Is that really what keeps you up at night?" Jack asked shoving him playfully

"No, what keeps me up all night is me and your mom getting it on" Bobby replied shoving back.

"Dude, that's your fucking aunt!" Jack bawled in disgust.

"So what, people do it in the south all the time." Bobby said teasingly. He lit a cigarette as they turned onto Yawkey Way.

"Why the fuck do you do that?" Jack asked.

"Do what?"

"Light your cigarette every time we're about to go into the park." Jack said pissed off.

"Who cares," Bobby said inhaling deeply and pointing at gate D, "There's no line anyway."

"That aint the point, we literally just walked all the way around the fucking baseball field and you decide to light up now?" Jack asked shaking his head.

"Relax and take in the scenery." Bobby replied nodding to a group of girls coming towards them.

Jack turned and smiled. "I like the way you think."

"Ladies," They both said at the same time bringing smiles to the girls' faces.

Bobby threw his cigarette on the ground and stomped it out as the girls walked by giggling. "Fucking waste, Eight bucks a pack and I didn't even finish." He said putting his arm around Jack. "You ready? Let's go watch some baseball."

They walked into the infamous baseball field, home of the Boston Fighting Cox, handing their tickets to the ticket collector. Bobby went first and immediately bee lined it to the beer vendor. There was a line, but not too bad.

Jack came up behind him and said, "Remember what I said."

Bobby turned around and clapped him on the back, "No worries, I wanna come back too. And besides, it would take about twenty of these things to make me slur my words and they're eight bucks a fucking beer." Jack gave him the eye that said *and?* "I only brought like forty bucks. Jesus Jack, could you please calm down?"

After they got their beer, two beers per customer per order limit, they went to their seats. The seats were four little wooden squares separated by little arm rests, on one side. On the other side there were four more identical seats. These two sections were separated by a huge iron railing that went all the way to the top of the section. An infant might be comfortable in these seats. Anyone over ten years old was going to engage in that inevitable battle over the armrest that has been going on since the park first opened.

Clay Buckley was on the mound for the Fighting Cox and AJ Burner for the Minutemen. They had the newest teen sensation singing the National Anthem. "I hate this fuck!" Bobby shouted and everyone laughed.

There were rarely any children in the section since it was mostly lifetime season ticket holders and Jack had to thank God for the little things.

He looked at Bobby and shook his head while he listened to the anthem of his beautiful country. They had a famous author from Maine throw the ceremonious first pitch and then the game got on.

Bobby got up after the second inning to go smoke. Where he sat was really uncomfortable and he was about to fight the guy next to him because, of course, they were fighting over the arm rest. The guy was so big that his fat was pouring into Bobby's personal area. He couldn't take it anymore and had to go for a walk.

There was a section outside where you could go smoke, but it was still a part of the park so you could go outside, smoke and get back in. They also had a couple of beer vendors and this is the main reason Bobby went out there. He knew how Jack felt about him getting drunk and he had said he only brought forty bucks, when in reality he had brought closer to three hundred.

He went to the Bud Light Vendor and held up two fingers. He took his beers a couple feet away knowing the vendor would forget his face almost instantaneously. It was impossible to remember people when you served a couple hundred beers an hour. He chugged both beers and went back. He held up two more fingers with a smile on his face. He walked a couple of steps to repeat the process hoping he could get good and drunk before going back to his seat.

He put the beer to his mouth as he watched the game on a huge screen they had plastered to the side of the building, when someone bumped into him spilling beer on his Becklet jersey.

"What the fuck?" He yelled and turned.

"Oh my God, I'm so sorry dude," The guy said and paused. "Sorry the Cox suck." He continued and laughed.

He was wearing a Minutemen shirt and a big grin on his face. Bobby could only see two other guys with him.

"Yea, he sucks real good just like your mom." Bobby chuckled and turned back to watch the screen.

He was taking a sip of his beer when the guy poured the beer he had in his hand over Bobby's head. The cold liquid was already getting sticky when Bobby was shoved so hard he hit a guy a few feet in front of him. The guy turned around and Bobby said, pointing at the Minutemen fan, "Sorry man this guy pushed me." The guy nodded and turned back around. Bobby turned to the Minutemen fan and asked, "Are you fucking retarded?"

"Retarded enough to beat your fucking ass." The guy replied.

"Uh huh, you're a Minutemen fan at the home of the Fighting Cox and you really want to fuck with me?" Bobby asked getting in the guys face with a scowl.

"Yea, so, what are you going to do about it?" The guy replied in a shaky voice. Wouldn't yours be if you'd just insulted the Fighting Cox at home all the while being a Minutemen fan?

Bobby turned around and handed his ticket and what was left of his beer to a girl who was taking in the action. "Take that darling," He said giving her his best sweet talker voice, "After all is said and done go sit in the seat that's on the ticket. You won't be disappointed, that, I can promise you."

He winked at her then turned back to the guy cocking back and swinging his fist. He connected good and solid where his father used to call the sweet spot, which was right under the chin. The guy went down and Bobby went down on top of him swinging both fists in practiced motion. His two friends tried to jump in but the surrounding Fighting Cox fans grabbed them. Bobby looked mad with hungry rage.

It took about two minutes for the cops to get there. There was zero tolerance for fighting ever since some little girl was hit with a bottle and killed during a huge brawl in the stadium. What the cops saw was a huge crowed chanting "Minutemen suck" in a circle. By the time they got to the middle the guy was unrecognizable and Bobby was unstoppable. One of the cops tried to grab Bobby's shoulder, but he just shrugged it off. Another cop grabbed his right hand but Bobby twisted it so the cop's grip broke. They finally decided to pull out a can of mace and let Bobby have it. That got him off the guy.

The cops formed a circle inside the center of the crowd and tried to push back what would eventually become an uncontrollable riot. The effort was met with a hail of boo's, but the cops were in control and kept pushing. Even though the crowd wasn't pleased with the break up they weren't hostile, yet, so they were easily dispersed.

The guy spit up blood along with a few teeth and tried to murmur something.

Bobby was escorted out of the park and he wore the same sick sadistic smile he had when he was beating the guy all the way to the paddy wagon.

The girl who Bobby gave the ticket to got back to the seats at the top of the fourth inning. "Um, that seats taken." Jack said as she sat next to him.

"If you mean by that guy who got arrested, he gave me the ticket and said to sit here. Wow these seats are insane. My sister is going to be so jealous when she sees this." She replied snapping photos with her phone.

"Wait a second what the fuck do you mean he got arrested?" Jack almost screamed.

"You're talking about the guy with short black hair and green eyes, really cute right?" She said like there wasn't a care in the world.

"Yea," Jack said shaking his head "Can you tell me what happened?" He asked trying not to lose his temper on this pretty girl he never seen in his life.

"So I was sitting in my shitty seats all the way in the bleachers." She said pointing to the bleacher seats. "I wanted to go smoke, so I went outside. I also wanted a beer so I got in line behind your friend. He got his beer and started watching the game on the screen that they have out there, you know, minding his own business. I started texting my sister telling her how hot he was when some guy bumped into him and said something. I don't know what it was because I couldn't hear him. Your friend told him that he sucked as good as his mom and turned back around. Then the asshole pushed him into another guy and poured his beer on him. Your friend then told him something, but I wasn't really paying attention. He handed me his ticket and a beer and a half and told me to come here when it was over then winked at me. He knocked the

12

guy down, then jumped on top of him and just punched the shit out of him, I mean when the cops dragged him off of the guy I thought he was dead until he spit out a couple of teeth. They were escorting your friend out when I came here. I seen a couple of cops asking some people questions."

"It's my cousin, that mother fucker, he should have known better." He replied on the verge of screaming. He wanted to lash out at this bitch for being able to say all this so nonchalantly. Not only would he lose the tickets, but he could probably kiss his job goodbye as well.

"Well, in your cousin's defense," She paused. "Well, that's what it was, self defense." She said giggling. "Also, the charges will be dropped."

"How do you know this?"

"Well, my father's a lawyer and I know for a fact that he can't be charged without enough people saying that he caused it. I'm pretty sure the Fighting Cox fans will stick up for him. Besides, they have cameras out there and can just watch it and see. You seem pretty upset that I'm here. What's wrong, am I not hot enough for you?" She asked flirtatiously.

"No it's not that." He said nervously.

She laughed. "I'm just kidding, your cousin will be fine so can you just relax and have a good time with me please?"

"I'm sorry. You are a very beautiful girl and I am honored to be in your presence." He said bowing his head.

"Aw, shucks, you're making me blush." She said sticking her hand out, "I'm Annabelle, but you can call me Anna."

"Jack." He replied taking her hand in his softly. "Is your sister going to be worried about you?" He was all of a sudden calm and realized Bobby was indeed thinking of him. If he wasn't then he wouldn't have given his ticket to someone else, a beautiful girl nonetheless.

"Nah, she called me a bitch. We came with a couple of friends, so she's not alone." She looked at him. "What your cousin did was awesome and sexy."

Jack shook his head knowing that only Bobby could beat someone to the brink of death and still be called sexy. "What are you doing after the game?"

She threw her arms up in a shrug. "You tell me Jack."

She started smiling a sexy smile. Her teeth were perfect. She made Jack fall in love right then and there. He was feeling good. His stupid cousin didn't get him in trouble and sent him this beautiful girl who he was going to hang out with after. On top of that the Fighting Cox won in extra innings with Pappelban closing. Jack didn't really care, however, the Fighting Cox weren't going to make the playoffs and with Anna here the game didn't seem so important.

Jack and Anna met up with Stacey, Anna's sister, and their friends, Lisa and Kerry, in the burger place near the subway station.

"So, Jack, what are we going to go do now?" Anna asked then took a bite of her cheeseburger.

"What do you want to do?" He asked.

"Let's get drunk." Anna kind of whispered looking around like it was a crime to do so and her friends all nodded their heads eagerly.

"Ok, where do you guys live?" He asked then thought about how much of a creep he sounded like. "I'm sorry, shit, what city I mean? I'm not a stalker or anything."

Anna chuckled and said, "Jack, you need to relax you're making me crazy. We live in Cambridge near Harvard Square." She replied trying to sound like a Bostonian by not pronouncing her 'R's.

"Sorry, Anna, you make me nervous, are you from Connecticut? Going off track, again I'm sorry. There's a bar I always go to in Somerville called Razzy's. I'm meeting my friends there if you want to come. It isn't too far from Harvard Sq," He said turning red with embarrassment, "Actually, it is, but we can give you a ride home or pay for your cab."

"Sounds like a plan." She said giving her friends a questioning look. They nodded and smiled.

They sat in the burger place for another half hour waiting for the foot traffic from the game to die down before they headed for Kenmore station to catch the train.

2

Bobby was sitting in the holding cell with two guys who were drunk and sleeping it off. The cell stunk of piss and homeless people and he wanted nothing more than a cigarette, but they told him they were keeping him until Monday when the courts opened, it was Friday.

He was hoping they would just bring him to the station and then let him off with a slap on the wrist, but he was resisting arrest and they could keep him on that alone. He just wanted to get the fuck out so he was playing nice guy.

He was hoping the girl he gave the ticket to told Jack what had happened, but he wasn't going to get his hopes up so he planned on staying in for the long haul. He thought about that girl and wondered if she even went to the seat. He wondered if Jack would have the balls to ask her out. He chuckled to himself thinking about the awkwardness that would go on.

He sat back and put his hands behind his head thinking he would try to get some sleep when he heard, "Release my fucking friend, you moron." His ears perked up at the sound of his friend Ronnie and he smiled.

Ronnie was getting in the officer's face. "You want to get arrested you fucking punk?" He asked pushing Ronnie away.

"You won't arrest me you clown." Ronnie replied being as arrogant a prick as he could.

"Really now and why won't I?" The cop asked sitting back down and folding his arms across his chest.

"My name, like I was trying to fucking tell you earlier, is Ronnie Harrington. My uncle is Jerry Harrington, you know, your boss."

"I don't believe you." The cop said sounding otherwise.

"Alright boss." He said pulling out his cell phone.

"You're bluffing."

"Are you sure about that, chief?" Ronnie asked smiling.

"Make the call." The cop said more composed.

Ronnie shrugged and dialed some numbers into his cell phone. "It's dialing, sailor."

"Stop calling me names." The cop said visibly agitated with Ronnie now.

Ronnie walked away for a few minutes and came back. "He's going to call you now. Have fun."

The phone rang and the caller ID said it was coming from the chief of police. Ronnie chuckled as the cop's look went from confident to straight out fear.

"Steve Downy," The cop stuttered into the phone. "Yes sir, right away sir." He hung up the phone. He gave a defeated look to Ronnie then scrambled to get Bobby.

"Don't you have to fill out paperwork or something?" Ronnie asked amused by the whole situation.

Steve gave him a look. "We never processed him."

"Wow and the shit just keeps piling up. I'll make sure to tell my uncle that you're a useless piece of shit." Ronnie said with confidence in his voice.

Steve didn't reply, he just put his head down and went through the locked door. He emerged a minute later with Bobby in tow. He gave Bobby his wallet and a couple of other affects he went in with.

Bobby looked through his wallet and laughed. "I had money in here."

"No you didn't." Steve replied.

"Are you trying to pocket my money you asshole?" Bobby asked livid.

"Stevie, do I have to call my uncle to have him come search you?" Ronnie asked pulling his cell phone back out. Steve reached in his pocket and pulled out money. "You're kidding me right?"

Steve didn't say anything, just put his head down. "What do you expect; guy's a piece of shit." Bobby said for him.

"I was gonna let the paperwork thing go, Steve, but now I'm just disgusted." Ronnie said shaking his head.

"You can't prove anything." He replied reaching for some sort of victory out of this travesty.

"Maybe not, but I'm pretty sure the camera recording us right now can." Ronnie said winking at him. "Let's get the fuck out of here Bobby I got to make a call." They started for the door and Ronnie turned back around, "I wonder what my uncle would think if he came to examine that video tape and there was a chunk of time missing out of it. Think about that and have a nice day."

"Jesus, fuck me, Christ!" Ronnie exclaimed as they were riding back to Razzy's. "You fucked that guy's shit up. What was going through your head?"Ronnie asked as they came to a stop light.

Ronnie's friends all called his van the pedophile mobile. It was dark blue and the only windows were the windshield and passenger and driver side window.

"Nothing," Bobby replied simply.

"You know how lucky you are?" Ronnie asked.

"Tell me Ron," Bobby replied absentmindedly

"Resisting arrest alone could have gotten you time, man. Thank God my uncle's the chief." Ronnie explained.

"How did you even know I was in there?"

"Jack texted me, man," Ronnie started, "He also told me you got some broad to sit with him in your place."

Bobby ignored him and turned up the radio. Metallica was blaring out with one of their long guitar solos. Bobby just watched the scenery as the light turned green and Ronnie took off. He just kept replaying the scenario over and over in his head, wondering if he could have handled it a little better. Probably not and he didn't feel bad for what he did. He was just nervous about what Jack was going to say to him. He didn't want his cousin to stop talking to him because some asshole thought he was tougher. Was Jack disappointed in him for fighting? Would he ever take him to another Fighting Cox game? These were the questions that rifled through his mind over and over like a recurring nightmare.

Jack was always worried when they went out together. Bobby was known for his quick temper and quicker fists. If anyone so much as looked at them wrong Bobby was swinging before Jack could blink. This often landed them on the cops' radar and as much as Jack hated fighting, Bobby's antics usually led to him fighting. Bobby still remembered the conversation they had when Jack finally admitted to not wanting to fight anymore.

It was after their senior prom at Somerville High School. One of the cheerleaders had brought a date from Everett High, Bobby hated Everett, and he started running his mouth about how Everett beat Somerville in football.

"Yea, we killed them this year. They thought they had a chance." The kid was telling one of Bobby's friends, laughing, while the last song played at the prom.

He ran and told Bobby after the prom was over, while Bobby was chugging a pint of Jim Beam in his limo saying, "He was calling you a pussy, Bobby."

There was a keg behind the high school later that night. This is where Bobby caught up with the kid. "I heard you were talking shit." Bobby said in a stern, but calm voice.

"About what?" The kid was asking clearly feeling a buzz.

"Playing stupid, huh? What the fuck did you say about me and the football team?"

"Oh, yea, you guys suck." The kid replied laughing without a care in the world.

"That's what I thought." Bobby smiled as four kids gathered behind the Everett kid; they were friends of his who showed up for the after party. Bobby grabbed the kid by his jacket and head butted him on the bridge of his nose. Jason, Ronnie, Nick and Jack were hitting the other ones before they could jump in.

It was after the fight when Jack confessed. "Bobby I can't do it anymore."

"Do what?"

"Beat people up. I feel bad."

Bobby started laughing thinking it was a joke, after all, they had grown up being taught how to fight.

"I'm not kidding. It eats me up inside." Jack said putting his head against the building. "You never looked into the eyes of a guy you just beat up and just felt bad?"

"Me, nah, but its cool, I mean, some people were born for it and others weren't. We keep this between us." Bobby replied handing him a bottle of Wild Turkey he'd taken from a liquor store. He chuckled softly and said "Me, feel bad, I never have and probably never will."

It was the last they talked about it. This is why Bobby was worried. He loved his cousin like a brother and didn't want him upset with him.

"We're here." Ronnie said, snapping Bobby out of his thoughts. "I'm warning you, there are people in there who are going to congratulate you. You seemed upset when I said something, so I thought you should have fair warning."

"Thanks," Bobby replied, but showed no signs of getting out of the van.

"Are you alright?" Ronnie asked killing the engine.

They were parked in the Conway Park parking lot, which was a park across the street from Razzy's. The outdoor hockey rink was filled with kids drinking beer and playing stickball. Bobby envied them for still being in high school with no worries. Bobby and his friends did the same not too long ago. The basketball courts were filled with kids shooting ball and other's on roller blades impatiently tapping sticks on the ground while they waited to use the rink, probably pissed to no end that the rink was being used as a stickball court instead of roller hockey, but speaking up would cause a fight. Oh how well Bobby, and Ronnie for that matter, knew those lives.

"I miss those days, man." Bobby said more to himself than to Ronnie.

"I know, but what are we gonna do? They aint invented time machines yet." Ronnie replied.

Bobby smiled at Ronnie and clapped him on the back. "You're a good friend. You've always been there for me and Jack. I love you, bro."

"Wow, are you going faggot?" Ronnie asked in a serious voice. "Dude you're my boy, but c'mon you can't expect me to go with you. I love pussy."

Bobby laughed. "I love you like a brother you clown. Let's go get smashed." He said getting out of the car. They were walking towards Razzy's and Bobby slowly put his hand in Ronnie's. Ronnie pulled his hand back freaked out and Bobby just laughed.

3

As they walked into Razzy's everyone started clapping. To the left was an arcade bowling game and to the right, the bar. Bobby went to order a pitcher, but there was one ready for him.

Ruth, the bartender said, "For you, drinks are on the house."

"Thanks Ruth, but that isn't necessary."

"It is, Bobby, it is," She said enunciating each word slowly, then jerked her head to the right, "Jack's in the back."

He smiled and said, "Thank you."

They walked passed the jukebox and bathrooms to the second room. It wasn't a private room, but not too many people had come back for karaoke yet, so it was pretty empty. Nancy, the owner, was bartending back here. Jack was at the first table to the left with four girls. Nick and Jason were sitting at the table next to them. As they started towards the table, Nancy called for Bobby. He handed the pitcher to Ronnie and went to the bar.

"Hey Nancy, how are you?" He asked sitting on the stool.

"Better after I heard what you did. It's about time somebody fucked up a Minutemen fan." She replied pouring two shots of whiskey. She gave him one of the shots then raised her own shot. She cut the music. "A toast!" she shouted over the loud conversations. "We don't always have something to celebrate, but tonight a toast to Bobby." Everyone cheered. Bobby lightly tapped his shot glass against Nancy's and they both downed them.

"Thanks Nancy, at least some people will appreciate what I did." Bobby said nodding his head towards Jack.

"I don't know about Jack, sweetheart," She said leaning over the bar, "but I'm proud of you."

Jack slid into the bar stool next to Bobby. "Two Bud lights please." He said holding up two fingers. Nancy turned the music back on and went to get the beers.

"But, we have a pitcher over there." Bobby said.

"Yea, we did, but now it's gone." He laughed.

"It wasn't there for a minute." Bobby replied shocked.

"Yea, well, what're you gonna do." Jack said shrugging.

"Listen, Jack, I'm sorry." Bobby started apologizing, but Jack held up a hand.

"You're my cousin and I love you. You do some of the stupidest shit I have ever seen sometimes. I asked you one thing. I was so pissed at the game, but Anna told me the story. I should be apologizing to you cuz."

"Anna? Wait what are you talking about, apologizing to me?" Bobby asked.

Nancy came back with the beers. "These are on the house boys."

"Thanks Nance." Jack replied. "Yea, Anna, the girl you gave your ticket to. I have to say that was genius by the way." He held his glass out to Bobby and Bobby clanked it.

"I was so worried you were gonna fuck shit up. Turns out, you actually did good this time."

"So you did have the balls." Bobby said chuckling. He felt the weight of the world leave his shoulders.

"Fuck you, asshole."

They walked back to the tables and sat down. Karaoke was about to start. "This is Anna, her sister Stacy and their friends Kerry and Lisa. This is Ronnie and the ever so popular Bobby." Jack said as he put his arm around Anna.

"Ladies." Bobby and Ronnie said in unison, tipping their glasses towards them.

"What are you gonna sing Bobby?" Stacey asked.

"Me? No I don't sing." He laughed.

"Oh yes you are cuz. If I have to than you have to. I already put us down, we're going up together." Jack said with a grin.

"What song?" Bobby asked kind of irritated. He knew he could never bow out of something his cousin said to do or he would look like a coward.

"Oh, you'll see." He started cracking up.

Bobby and Ronnie needed to play catch up so they started pounding beers. Bobby drinking faster to get rid of his nerves and it worked. They were on their fifth pitcher between the two of them when they were called up.

Bobby was pretty drunk by this point. He grabbed a mic and looked at the blurry screen then at the crowd, who were waiting to laugh. As the lyrics came up he started singing, "Is this the real life? Is this just fantasy? Caught in a landslide, no escape from reality."

After they were finished singing their horrible version of Bohemian Rhapsody, the crowd clapped and cheered. It made Bobby's drunken confidence shoot up. Jack looked at his cousin and smiled. They were having a great time.

After a few hours their group kind of split up and Jack got to talk to Anna alone. Because he was drunk, he didn't care about embarrassing himself so he kept asking her questions. He learned Anna was going to MIT on scholarship for tennis. She got straight A's, but was one of the most outgoing girls he'd ever met. He told her about his tire job and how he was trying to get the assistant manager position.

They were sitting in the booth when Nancy came with a tray full of shots. "Hey, Bobby, some girl bought these for you and your friends."

"Really, Nance, who was it?" Bobby asked excitedly.

"I don't know I didn't get a good look and I think she already left." Nancy said and then turned and walked away.

Jason started laughing as he took a shot glass and held it up, "To Bobby, I have never drunk so much in my life for free." He said slurring a little.

"Fuck you. Drink up, bitch, cause were gonna do four more rounds after this. What is it anyway?" Bobby asked. "Smells like tequila." Stacey said making a face.

After all the shots were gone, Bobby went up to Nancy and held all of his fingers up. "Can we get thirty six more?"

"Jesus Christ, Bobby," She said handing him the bottle, "Just fucking take it and don't get alcohol poisoning."

As he brought the bottle back to the table some girl handed him a piece of paper. "Call me." She said then turned and left. He shrugged to himself and chuckled.

"Aren't you the stud?" Anna asked laughing.

"It's crazy, I almost killed someone and for some reason I'm everyone's fucking hero. It's like I just got back from Iraq or something." He said shaking his head.

"Girls love a badass." She said downing a shot.

The liquor was flowing and Bobby felt darkness take him over as he blacked out. Last thing he remembered was talking to some girl about how he was black from the waist down.

Jack would also succumb to this darkness but not before he declared his love for Anna. He was supposed to be singing Endless Love to her, but everything came out in gibberish screeches, so instead of singing he just repeated over and over that he was in love with her.

Ronnie and Nick were both hitting on Stacey, very unsuccessfully I might add.

Jason was on stage dancing with a speaker in the corner.

Kerry stumbled into the wall, fell down and then passed out.

Lisa was watching Jason with tears streaming down her cheeks, because she was laughing so hard.

Everyone was having such a good time that Nancy kept the back room open for another two hours.

4

"Where the fuck am I?" Bobby asked to nobody in particular as he tried to sit up, but the room started spinning and he immediately fell back down.

"Shh," Replied the naked girl lying next to him. "My head is pounding. We're in a room."

Bobby looked at the girl smiling. It wasn't the girl whom he told he had a big dick. It was Stacey. She was hot and her body was outrageous. He knew they had sex, because he had the used condom on still.

"How did we get here?" Bobby asked trying to piece together what he missed, but she was already sleeping again. He sat there and admired the way her light brown hair slightly covered her face.

He slowly pushed up on his elbows and looked around. To the left was another bed with two people in it. Next to that was a window with a computer to the right of that. Next to the computer was a pink chair, then a couple of portable closets and stacked plastic bins. On the wall across from him was a 42" flat screen TV hanging on the wall with a DVD rack underneath. That wall led to a door about ten feet away.

He got out of bed, took the rubber off and stretched. His insides felt like they were on fire and head felt like he'd been hit with a bat, but at least the room stopped spinning.

"Yup, I'm definitely hung over." He muttered to himself as he pulled his boxer briefs and jeans back on. He started towards the bathroom and tripped over a body. He looked down to see Jason and Nick hugging each other and then Lisa and Kerry, each with a hand on Ronnie's bare chest.

Ronnie was moaning from Bobby kicking him in the head, but then he fell back asleep.

Bobby walked through the door which led into a living room and kitchen combination. The bathroom was to the left and to the right of that was the front door. The roommate's room was directly across which was probably identical to the room he was just in. He walked into the bathroom, which was full of pink girly shit, and turned on the cold water and let it sit for a few seconds before splashing it in his face. That's when he heard screams. He ran back into the bedroom and seen Jason and Nick staring at each other in horror. He started laughing, "Looking in each other's eyes like intimate lovers?"

"Fuck you man!" Nick retorted harshly.

"Yea, this shit aint funny dude." Jason added.

"Fuck my life." Ronnie said sitting up as quickly as he dared, which wasn't very quick at all. He looked at both girls on either side and smiled. Then he looked at Nick and Jason and his smile widened, "Better yet, fuck your life, mine's just fine." He stood up and walked to the bathroom. His piss lasted at least two minutes leaving everyone in an awkward silence.

"Was he good, Nick?" Jack asked rising up from his peaceful slumber.

"Really, are you serious? Come on nothing happened!" Nick almost screamed.

Anna rose with a smile. She rubbed Jack's naked chest. "I think you made me fall in love with you last night." She raised her arms in a stretch forgetting she had no shirt on. When she realized her breasts were there for everyone to see, she quickly covered up with the blankets.

Lisa and Kerry both woke up with sleep crusted eyes and asked, "What happened?" almost simultaneously. They, however, were not nude, which Bobby found made him upset.

Ronnie came into the room then and smiled, "I don't know, but I hope it was awesome."

They looked at Anna for questions, but she just shrugged. Stacey rose almost identically as her sister did, but she wasn't as shy and left her bare tits out like she was in a girl's locker room. "Can we go to get pancakes?" She asked while every guy in the room just stared.

Bobby looked at his cell phone and seen he had two missed calls from a number he didn't know and one voice message. He hit the button that connected him to voice mail and listened to a pissed off voice definitely from New York.

"Hey you little faggot cunt! My name is Jackie G and that guy you smashed up is my fucking cousin. I want to set up a meet so I can kill you. Don't bother ignoring me either you piece of shit. Think about it, if I found your number, I can find you. Tell your little bitch cousin to get ready cause he's going to get it too. Call this number back and we'll set up that meet. I think you should be a man" Then the automated voice came on telling him to press one to repeat, which he did and handed the phone to Jack. Everyone was looking back and forth between Jack and Bobby, except Jason, who was still staring at Stacey's tits. Both Bobby and Jack had a glazed look on their faces. Finally he hung up.

"Do you think its mob?" Jack asked in a nervous voice.

"How the fuck should I know? I'm calling him back just in case." Bobby said and left the room. He had no idea where he was going, but needed to get away from everyone else.

Everyone stood quiet after Bobby left for what seemed like an eternity. Ronnie was the one who finally broke the silence. "Ok, I guess I'll say what I'm pretty sure everyone else is thinking. What the fuck!" He almost screamed in both fear and confusion. "I mean, Jack, how the fuck did we get here? What the fuck happened? Who the fuck is Bobby going to call? Why are Nick and Jason holding each other?" He continued to rifle questions at Jack until he finally put up his hand in a stop motion.

"Shut the fuck up, please, and let me think for a second." Jack answered. Everyone stayed quiet, but he wasn't thinking he just didn't want to listen to anyone. His head was pounding and all he wanted was an aspirin and more sleep.

"You know what Bobby reminded me of that I forgot to tell you guys?" Anna said

"What's that sweetheart?" Jack replied, slowly massaging his temples.

"A hooligan,"

"What are you talking about?" Jack asked.

"You know, like from the movie *Green Street Hooligans*" She said chuckling, but Ronnie and Jack gave each other a blank stare. "None of you saw it?" She asked shocked. They all shook their heads.

"Is it good?" Nick asked.

"Everyone grab a seat. We need to watch this." Anna said smiling.

"What about your roommate?" Jack asked.

"Nah, don't worry about her she's never here. She only comes like once a month or so, but mostly she stays with her boyfriend." She replied and gave Stacey a look.

As they grabbed seats and started the movie Bobby was exiting the apartment building onto Mass Ave. He looked around to get his bearings right, then took out his phone and looked at the missed calls. Bobby feared nothing on this planet, but for some reason when he hit the call button his hand was shaking.

"Hello." A deep New York accented voice answered.

"Jackie G?" Bobby almost stuttered.

There was a chuckle. "No, hold on a minute Bobby." For some strange reason Bobby felt naked on Mass Ave. in the middle of heavy foot traffic as he waited for, what seemed like forever. Finally he heard some fidgeting on the other end.

"Bobby, Bobby, Bobby. What the fuck am I gonna do with you my man?"

"Just one question Jackie. Are you connected?"

There was another chuckle, "No, just a pissed off cousin. So when and where do you want to meet?"

"I don't know why you want to meet!" Bobby yelled into the phone drawing attention to him from the pedestrians. His confidence was back. He composed himself and started again. "Really, your cousin started it. He got in my face."

"Let me ask you this, what would you do if it was your cousin Jack in the hospital bed?"

"Wait, how do you know who my cousin is?"

"Just answer the question Bobby."

He sighed, "I would probably kill someone, now answer my question. How do you know my cousin?"

"See you and I are a lot alike. Because I'm probably gonna kill you. It doesn't matter who starts it and you know it."

"Maybe, but that still doesn't answer my fucking question you asshole. How do you know my cousin?" Bobby said slowly, trying his hardest not to throw his phone as hard as he could.

"Oh, I know a lot. I may not be connected, but I know people who know people. Call me when you figure out when and where we meet," There was a pause and then, "And do make it soon, I'd hate to have to go find you because you're being a coward."

Bobby sat there listening to the dial tone for five minutes trying to figure out what the hell just happened.

There he stood, shirtless and bare footed as people walked all around in heavy foot traffic and for the first time in his life he felt so insignificant.

Bobby walked back to the apartment and knocked. The door was unlocked, but his head was somewhere else, which is why he didn't hear them yelling to come in. Finally Nick ripped the door open, "What the fuck dude!" Bobby just brushed passed him without a word. "Dude?" Nick called, but Bobby just walked into the bedroom.

At that moment Pete Dunham was putting a rival hooligan's head through a tipped over phone booth. "Jack." He said and walked back into the living room. Jack regretfully took his arm away from Anna and jumped up.

"What's wrong?" He asked as he walked out of the room and shut the door.

"I just called the number. Not mob, but has friends. He knows us and will come after us if I don't set up a meet."

"So, what's the problem? Set one up."

"They'll probably kill me, but you're right."

"Don't worry, I'll be there," He pinched Bobby's cheek playfully, "and don't worry I wont let the bad men hurt you."

"I don't want you involved in this Jack. This is my mess, not yours." He replied smacking his hand away.

"Fuck that, dude, I'm fighting with you."

"Me too," Nick said from behind them. Bobby completely forgot about him.

"None of you are going to fight. I'll call him back and take a beating. Don't worry its cool."

Jack shook his head and opened the door, "We're watching this movie called *Green Street Hooligans* and I'm going to finish it. I suggest you watch it with us and after that we'll figure this mess out."

He turned and walked in the room with Nick right behind him. Bobby slowly walked in and saw Stacey telling him to sit in bed with her with her finger movement. He sat on the bed and she pulled him down and they cuddled through the whole movie, but Bobby wouldn't focus, no, he had other things on his mind.

5

Bobby sent a text out to Jackie. *I will meet up with you, but no weapons and it has to be where I say. I will be alone so you don't need to get Jack involved.*

He wasn't focused on the conversation. Something about figuring out what happened last night. Bobby was in his own head even when Jack was trying to get his attention. Finally Stacey elbowed him and got his attention.

"What?" He asked as if he was still in school and the teacher picked him to answer a question, but he wasn't paying attention.

"What the fuck is going on in that head of yours?" Jack asked.

"Nothing man, I'm just tired that's all."

"Bullshit. You're going to that fight alone aren't you?" He could read his cousin like a book after all these years.

"Jack, these are my demons. I'm the fighter, you're a good kid let it go."

"Fuck you I'll come." Jack replied as stubborn as Bobby.

Bobby's phone went off as they walked into diner that served breakfast and lunch. There was nobody in the place, so they were immediately seated. He'd forgotten to put it on vibrate. *Well I'm at Mass General with my cousin now so you tell me when and where.*

Bobby had thought long and hard about the where. He knew the when would have to be night time, but as to where, he had a million places he thought of. He had to reject all of them except one, due to the lack of seclusion.

There was a soccer field behind Kmart where Jack's father used to take them fishing when they were younger. This would be his best bet. It would be hard for anyone to see them from the parking lot, unless they walked to the edge of the field. And cops rarely patrolled the area.

There's a Kmart in Assembly Sq in Somerville. Look to the back, you'll see a cab station. Follow that road to the parking lot where there is a soccer field. I'll be midfield waiting. He looked at the clock; it was already two in the afternoon. *Midnight, remember no weapons.*

"You're meeting tonight?" Jack said more than asked.

"I love you cuz, but I got to do this myself." He stood up and pulled his wallet out. "You guys have a great evening. Breakfast is on me. It was very nice to have made your acquaintance ladies." He threw a hundred that he knew he shouldn't spend and walked out into the unforgiving sunlight.

"We didn't even order!" Jack tried to call after him, but Bobby was gone.

"You're just gonna let him leave!" Anna exclaimed.

"Yea, come on man, what the fuck. We can't let him do this alone." Ronnie added.

"Don't worry. I know my cousin like a book. Right now he's hung over as shit. He'll need rest so he's going back to the apartment to take a nap. He won't think of deleting his text messages and so we can go in with the keys he leaves everywhere and have a look. His phone will be on the kitchen table charging so we won't wake him." He looked at his watch and signaled to the waiter, "Now let's order breakfast, we got plenty of time."

"Ok. That settles that. Now, the question of the day is where the fuck is my van?" Ronnie replied.

"It's still at Razzy's. Kerry wouldn't let you drive. That much I remember." Stacey said.

"Is that true?" Ronnie asked and she nodded, "Well then you truly are my hero." Ronnie smiled and Kerry blushed.

"Now, as for The Bean Street Hooligans," Jack started.

"Wait, no absolutely not!" Anna almost screamed.

"What?" Jason replied.

"This retard wants to start a hooligan gang for the Fighting Cox. I won't allow it!"

"First of all, how in the hell do you know that, and second of all, I'm going to do it. It would be awesome. Think of how many Fighting Cox fans there are in America. We wouldn't lose!"

"But if you do this you would be Pete. He fucking dies!" She yelled on the verge of tears.

"Why are you so emotional? You barely know me, but you act as if we're married. Besides Bobby would be Pete, right guys?" There were nods all around the table from the guys.

"I told you. Last night you made me fall in love with you, I wasn't joking." She looked away embarrassed.

He grabbed her chin and made her look into his eyes. "Nothing will happen to me. I got these guys and you saw what Bobby can do. What do you say we go on a date after we help Bobby, just me and you?"

She pulled her head away and looked from Ronnie to Jason and then to Nick. "If he gets a scratch I'll kill you all. Tell Bobby too. I'm not playing." She looked at Jack. "I would love a date. Where are we going?"

"How about bowling? Ronnie can I use your van?"

"Sure, once we get it." Ronnie said impatiently.

They walked the girls back to the apartment and Jack promised to hang out with Anna before the fight tonight instead of after.

When they got to her steps, Jack grabbed Anna and kissed her deeply. She pulled away and looked in his eyes. "Ask me."

"Ask you what?"

"Ask me to be your girlfriend. I have never been asked. My dad was very protective so boys stayed away. So ask me god dammit!"

Jack got on one knee and looked up into her eyes. "Anna, will you be my girlfriend?"

A small crowd drew around them. She threw her hands up to her face with fake shock. "Oh my goodness Jack, This is so sudden! Of course I will!" She exclaimed and threw her arms around him. They kissed while everyone clapped and cheered. To their knowledge, these two strangers had just gotten engaged.

When they got to Ronnie's van it had a $50 ticket for overnight parking. Ronnie looked at the ticket and said, "They tell you not to drive drunk and then give you a fucking ticket when you don't? Jesus Christ."

"Fuck it, let's go, he should be asleep, but I'll text him near Tufts just in case." Jack said.

"Were you serious earlier?" Nick asked hesitating.

"You talking about that thing with Anna. That was just fun bullshitting." He replied grabbing the handle to the door.

"No, he's not talking about that." Jason replied.

"What the hell are you guys talking about?" Jack asked confused

"When you said you wanted to start the firm." Ronnie said.

"Yea, why wouldn't I be serious?"

"It's just that, we know how you feel when Bobby fights." Ronnie said.

"I'm dead serious, but if you guys don't want to do it then I'd understand." Jack said getting angry and defensive.

"You know us, Jack, we're all down for whatever, but we just want to make sure you know what you're getting into." Jason said.

"Listen, guys, my life has been boring for awhile now and maybe this will make it better. Also Anna got wet over that guy in the movie, trust me I felt it." He said grinning.

"Ok, we just wanted to make sure. Let's go help your dumb cousin out." Jason replied jumping in the van.

Bobby lived in the apartment building at 148 on High St. in Medford. There was an entry door only accessible by key or ringing a doorbell. Once you were in here you had access to the whole building except the apartments themselves. He lived in a one bedroom on the first floor.

He had taken Nightquil and passed out setting his alarm clock for 8 pm. He didn't want anyone to bother him so he put his phone on silent, which, as Jack suggested, was on his kitchen table.

Bobby was always losing his keys and was sick of paying the fines to have the building super let him in and then give him a copy. He kept the entry door key above the entry door header and his apartment key above his apartment door header. He knew anyone had access to his place, but he thought the chances of someone finding both keys were slim.

Only a few people knew about the keys and those few were getting out of a parked van in front of his apartment building.

Jack felt above the header and grabbed the key, "Good old predictable Bobby." He smiled.

He unlocked the door and put the key back in place making sure no one saw. They walked into the hall and for some reason; they decided to tiptoe all the way to Bobby's door even though the hallway was deserted. Jack felt above the header one more time and smiled again grabbing hold of the key.

He turned the key and they walked in quietly. To the right Bobby was in his bedroom snoring away. In front of them was his bathroom. They walked through the big living room on the left and into the kitchen straight ahead. It was so narrow that Jack had no idea how Bobby fit his 3'X5' kitchen table with three chairs.

He grabbed the phone and looked at texts. He erased the one he had sent once they hit Tufts and found the one about meeting behind Kmart at midnight under a random number.

When they were safely at the van Jack said, "We got time. You should go get sleep."

"What are you gonna do?" Nick asked.

Jack smiled. "Go be with my new girlfriend."

They got in the van and Jack dialed her. "Hey baby, are you alone?"

"No, Jack, I have to be honest with you now that we're officially together," She said pausing long enough for Jack to imagine a million different possibilities, none of which made him feel good, "We all live here. We lied to you guys just in case we didn't like you." She giggled innocently.

"You're bad. You need a spanking. How about we come get you and you can come back to my place and we can rent a movie. I think I'd rather do that then go bowling."

"That sounds good." She replied and he could imagine her grinning ear to ear through the phone. God he loved that smile.

Ronnie dropped everyone off then drove to his house. Jack was confused. "Dude what are you doing?"

"Listen, you and Bobby, you guys are family and I'm down for whatever, so I'll be there. We need to be stealthy. Think that over and while I'm in bed I'll try to think of a plan. In the mean time you can take the van, just call when you pick everyone up." He jumped out and walked into his house. Bobby looked at the clock; it was now 3:30 PM. He took off back towards Mass Ave.

When she jumped in she looked at him with puppy dog eyes. "I'm sowry I wied. I wuv you."

He smiled. "Stop, I don't care. What movie do you want to watch?"

"Well," she replied. "Since you're so adamant about doing this I thought you should study. I brought *Green Street Hooligans* again. This time pay attention."

Jack still lived with his parents in the basement of 114 Moreland St in Somerville. It was a basement apartment and they treated him like a tenant so he had his privacy. He paid three hundred dollars a month and even though his parents still paid for everything else, including food, cable and toiletries, he still felt independent.

The only entrance was from the back of the house. It wasn't a white picket fence type of house, but it was single family and although the Mystic projects were right around the corner, it was a decent neighborhood.

He opened a big steel door which led them into a kitchen area. He didn't really clean, but it wasn't messy. He had a few dishes in the sink from his last meal. Overall, Anna thought he was a neat person.

To the left was his bedroom which had a sliding door. To the right was a laundry and bathroom with a stand up shower. Both were divided by a wall that ran the length of the entire basement.

His bedroom was surprisingly big for the space he had down there. There was a king size bed with a few dressers and there was still room for her to lie on the floor and spread her arms out. He had a dark green rug in there and a Fighting Cox emblem on one wall and a shamrock on another wall. The rest was painted white. The TV was a 32" flat screen hanging off the wall across from the bed. There was a dresser in the back behind the bed going across the whole wall and one under the TV, which wasn't as big. There was a PS3 on top of that dresser. The DVD rack was to the left. Anna looked and seen one whole row devoted to porn.

She looked up at his red face and smiled. "Well, at least it's all straight and no creepy stuff."

He relaxed and smiled. "The creepy stuff is in my closet."

She looked around, "There is no closet."

"I know, let me see the movie." He took it and put it in the PS3 as she undressed. "I thought you wanted to watch this?" He said with mock agitation.

"I do, where are your T-shirts?" She replied.

He pointed to the dresser against the back wall, "Lower drawer in the middle."

She took out a Highlanders long T with a football logo over the heart. "You played football?"

"Yea, I was a tight end. Bobby played too. He was a linebacker." He pointed to a photo on the dresser of them in their football uniforms.

"You guys are really close huh?" She asked.

"You know how a lot of kids grow up with older brothers or sisters to look out for them?" She nodded. "Well, I didn't have one so Bobby kind of took on the roll of older brother."

"Aren't you guys the same age?" She asked.

"Yea, well, that didn't mean he didn't always have my back. Even when I told him not to, but that's just how Bobby is. I remember one time when we were playing basketball down the park. We were with one of my friends, Mike, who Bobby didn't even know. Someone started a fight with Mike and Bobby jumped in when it was clear my friend had had enough. You see, Bobby always believed in a fair fight, but when it's clearly over, then that means it's over. We were ten. Bobby ripped the kid off of Mike and threw him to the ground. He went to help Mike up when the kid pushed Bobby from behind and he tripped over Mike. Bobby got up shaking and said, 'I wasn't gonna kill you, but now you should run.'" Jack laughed at the memory. "The kid stood his ground, which impressed me anyways, so Bobby tackled him and just started laying punches into his face. By the time we got Bobby off of him, the kid was out cold. His breathing was choked, like he was dying. We were the only people around so we grabbed Bobby and ran.

"I found out later that the kid was in a coma for a couple of weeks and when he woke up he wasn't right. They ran a bunch of test and found out that he was retarded. I never told Bobby though. I always thought the kid kind of deserved it, like if Bobby didn't stop him he would have killed my friend." He gave her a weak smile.

"Oh my God, Jack. That's awful." She said not so much disgusted with Bobby's actions as shocked that Jack would have seen this at such a young age.

"The thing about Bobby that you need to understand is that he always fought for the little guy. He always wanted to be a super hero. Like when he wrote papers about what he wanted to be when he grew up, it was always about being like Superman or Batman. I know for a fact that when he was seven he would roam the streets in a mask looking for villains to defeat." He chuckled again. "As we got older, though he kind of lost sight of being a super hero and kind of just fought."

She saw the sadness in his eyes. She lay down and patted the bed next to her, "Come hold me and let's watch the movie."

He pressed play on the PS3 remote and did as he was told. "I never told anyone any of that so that stays between us, ok?"

She turned around and kissed his lips, "Of course. Jack?"

"Yea,"

"Is it weird that I think I'm already in love with you after only knowing you for a day?"

"Well if you're weird, then so am I."

They started making out and Jack pulled away. "I thought you wanted me to study?"

"Session's over." She replied and started undressing him.

6

Bobby woke up to his alarm going off. He had overslept a half hour. He jumped up and ran to the kitchen to check his phone, for some reason he thought he missed the meet, and seen a text message from a number he didn't know. He opened it. *Bobby, please don't go by your self. It's Stacey. Call me.* He ignored it and jumped in the shower.

After he got out he grabbed his phone and seen he had a missed call. It was Stacey again. He put the ringer on and scrolled down to the number and pushed the call button. She answered immediately "Bobby?"

"Yes. What's going on Stacey?"

"I don't know what you're doing tonight, but please take your friends."

"It's ok Stacey, I'll be fine. Just go out and I'll call you later."

"You're making me worry, Bobby."

"It's ok, I promise." He hung up before she could say another word.

He went to his closet and thought about what he should wear. The nights were starting to get chilly, but he didn't want to wear jeans to a fight. He picked out a gray pair of sweats and decided on his black T-shirt that had Boston at the top, the Fighting Cox logo in the middle and then the word Fighting Cox at the bottom, his white sneakers and a light gray zip up hooded sweatshirt.

He sat on his couch and impatiently waited for quarter of midnight, since Kmart was a 5 minute drive away from his apartment, he didn't need a lot of time to get there.

He was nodding off by the time it came around; the Nyquil was still in his system. He went into is bedroom and opened his closet. He had a cheap set of plastic drawers his aunt had bought him one year and this is where he kept his weapons hidden. He took out two pairs of brass knuckles and put them in either pocket of the hooded sweatshirt. He took one last look around his apartment like it was going to be his last and walked into the hall. He reached up for the key and locked his door then put the key back slowly, with a longing feeling. He didn't know why he felt this would be the end, but the feeling was so strong that it was making him nauseous.

He owned a 2001 Nissan Maxima. He jumped in it and took off, second guessing his decision to bring his car, since he was still paying for it and didn't want it to get messed up by Jackie G. In the end he didn't really care.

He drove towards Medford Sq and stayed on that road all the way, driving as slow as he could taking in every scene he could. He really thought this was his last night on earth.

He took a right on Fellsway going south. He proceeded to drive over the Mystic River and went into the left lane for the shopping center. He followed the road to Kmart. He took a left and followed the road all the way to the back and parked his car. He got out and walked to the midfield and waited just as he said he would.

When Jack woke up from his nap he called Ronnie, Nick and Jason. He told them to be ready, because he would pick them up soon. He told Anna he would see her in a little while and kissed her on the head. She mumbled and rolled over never really waking up.

After he picked everyone up they parked in the Kmart parking lot at the back.

"You figure out a plan, because I got nothing," Ronnie said.

"Ok so Right now it's exactly midnight." He looked at his phone to confirm. "So they should be there now. I figure they'll talk shit to each other for a few minutes. We should park in front of the boat yard and walk over. They chant shit in the movies so I figure we should too right?"

"You're serious about this shit?" Nick asked.

"Definitely, so, anyway, how about Minutemen suck? Seems fitting right?" He smiled big. He loved the idea of a hooligan gang and it wasn't even because it turned Anna on anymore.

"Whatever, man, so we run out chanting Minutemen suck and hit someone?" Jason asked losing patience.

"Exactly," Jack pointed to him.

Ronnie jumped In the driver's seat and started towards the boat yard. It was now five past midnight and he prayed to God Jack was right about the talking shit part.

Unfortunately, for Bobby, he was wrong. Right after he hit midfield, Jackie G put his car in park. Eight guys jumped out of his SUV including him and they all walked towards Bobby. Bobby never heard the car park, or the doors slam. He was looking at the bridge that runs over the Mystic for the Orange line.

He turned as Jackie's fist connected with his eye. It swelled shut instantly. Another guy kicked his knee in sending him down like he was about to be knighted.

"Not as tough as I would have thought after seeing what you did to Jimmy." Jackie G yelled.

"Who is," Bobby started, but Jackie hit him in the face again. Bobby fell to the ground and was instantly met with a melee of boots. He was kicked in the stomach and ribs, but thankfully nothing broke. He was kicked in the nuts and back. He was kicked in the face and back of his head.

After Bobby thought he was going to pass out from the pain he heard a "Minutemen suck!" chant. Through blurred vision in the only eye he could see out of, he saw four shapes sprinting towards them.

"What the fuck?" One of Jackie's associates asked, but he would get no answer. Jack swung a bat connecting with the guys head. He went down instantly. Nick kicked one guy in the balls then punched another guy in the face, knocking them both down. Jason took out some guy's knees with a lead pipe. The guy Nick kicked in the nuts was trying to get up, but Ronnie came out of nowhere with a haymaker sending the guy into a world full of dreams.

"Now it's fair, four on four." Jack said as he squared up with Jackie G. They both took a boxing stance. Jackie threw a jab and connected with Jack's stomach. Bobby tried to get up and fight, but the intense pain in his ribs wouldn't let him do anything but lay there and suffer.

Jackie tried a haymaker, which Jack ducked. He came up hard with an uppercut lifting both him and Jackie off their feet. To Bobby it looked like a move from the street fighter video game.

Nick squared up with a guy who was easily twice his size, but Nick was an experienced boxer. The guy swung at him, but was clumsy and slow. Nick dodged it easily and went straight for the guy's kidney with a four punch combo sending the guy to his knees. The guy got up and tried to regain his balance. Amused, Nick allowed him to get it. He tried to throw another haymaker. Nick bent back dodging it again and jumped forward with and elbow breaking the guy's nose. The guy went down to his knees and Nick punted him in the face as hard as he could which knocked him out.

Ronnie took his man by the shirt and just started head butting him until the guy was limp in his hands. He dropped the guy and ran to Bobby, who was moaning in pain and said, "You're alright buddy. Sorry we didn't get here sooner man."

The last guy started crying and fell to his knees. "I'm sorry man! I just did what Jackie asked, that's all!" Jason shrugged to Jack who shrugged back.

Jack walked over and looked at the guy and said, "Not so tough when it's evenly matched, huh? Don't worry, we won't hit you, but you will tell Jackie that we're the Boston Fighting Cox Hooligans. If he was smart, he would start one for the Minutemen. Tell him to spread the word. Every time Boston plays another team, we'll be there to fight whether or not they want to fight back."

He walked to Ronnie and helped him get Bobby to his feet. Bobby screamed in pain as they lifted him. "Do you think anything is broken?" Ronnie asked.

"No, I don't think so just bruised. I told you to let me deal with this myself." Bobby said his voice barely above a whisper.

"You're welcome." Jack said turning his head. "Hey Nick can you call Stacey? Anna told me she's getting her nursing license soon. Ask if she can come over and have a look at our hero."

Nick took out his phone and made the call. Jason took Ronnie's keys and ran to get the van.

Jackie G and his crew were moaning and rolling around the ground, except for the guy who was crying.

They carried Bobby to the van as Nick hung up the phone and said, "She can come, but she needs a ride. She owns a bike, but thinks that'll take too long. Also, I think she was crying."

"Ok I'll take Bobby's car and go pick up Stacey. Bobby, where are your keys?"

"They're in the ignition." Bobby replied weakly.

"I hope you didn't lock the fucking door." Jack said.

"Me too," He replied.

"Ok, make sure he gets to bed and I'll come back as soon as I can." Jack said barking out orders.

Ronnie started laughing and said, "You sat at breakfast, looked Anna in the eyes and said you weren't playing Pete

Dunham's role. Yet here you are barking out orders playing the Major."

"Fuck off." Jack replied in an English accent.

"I think it should be piss off, not fuck off, bro." Ronnie replied laughing harder.

Jason pulled up in the van and Jack helped them load Bobby into the back then he ran over to the Maxima, which was unlocked, and drove away.

7

When he was in front of Stacey's building he called her and before it rang twice, she was already in the back seat with Lisa. Kerry jumped up front. Jack could tell that Stacey had been crying. "What are they doing here?" He asked.

"They're here for your protection." She said almost growling.

Jack put the car in drive and pulled off of the curb chuckling. "No I'm serious."

"I am too. You know, you're a fucking asshole. When you promised Anna that you would be ok, that was only you? Why didn't you protect Bobby?" She almost screamed, the tears rising in her eyes again.

"Stacey, relax, he's ok. If we didn't get there, then he would have gone to the morgue instead of his bed." Jack replied sympathetically. He looked in the rear view mirror and seen Lisa hugging her. "I'm not trying to sound like a dick, but you just met him. I mean did you guys even have a conversation before you,"

"Hey Jack what year is this?" Kerry asked and started shaking her head.

"The Maxima, um, it's a 2001." He replied confused. He looked in the rearview again and either Stacey didn't hear him or chose not to. He looked back at Kerry and she mouthed the words I'll tell you later. Jack just nodded more confused then ever, so he just turned up the music and drove back to Bobby's.

When they were walking up to the front door Jack noticed a bag on Stacey's shoulder that he hadn't seen before. "What's in there?" He asked as he rang the doorbell, apparently Bobby decided to bring his keys in this time, only meaning to start a friendly conversation.

As they were buzzed in she rolled her eyes and said, "My nursing supplies, dickhead." Then she cringed as they could hear Bobby moaning as soon as they stepped foot in the building. She gave Jack a menacing look and started towards the sound. She had never been to his apartment before, but she followed his moans and came to the right apartment.

When they walked in Ronnie was helping Bobby back to bed. Nick and Jason were playing the PS3. Jack looked at them with questioning eyes.

"Oh, he had to take a piss. Good news, no blood." Nick said. Stacey ignored him and went into the bedroom.

"Ok, I have to go see Anna, I'll be back soon. Don't let him up!" He exclaimed to them. Ronnie came out a few seconds later looking sad. "What's going on?" Jack asked nervously.

"She kicked me out man. What the fuck?" He replied with his head down.

Jack shook his head and walked out. Kerry followed him to the walkway outside. "Jack, I don't know what's wrong with her or Anna for that matter. I've seen them with guys before, but never like this. Something happened to them last night and now they're both in love with you guys. I stopped you from finishing your sentence because you were about to make an asshole out of yourself. She told me she loved him and didn't know why. She wants to get to know him but," She put her arms up in a shrugging motion, "you can't fight feelings, right?"

Jack looked slowly at the building, knowing exactly what she meant, then back at her. "Thank you Kerry. You think you and Lisa could do me a favor?" She nodded. "You think you could keep those retards in there busy while Stacey checks out Bobby?" She nodded again and smiled before she went back towards the building. Jack watched her go in and started for the car.

Stacey told Ronnie to get the fuck out, and then looked at Bobby. "Jesus Christ. I told you to bring them! Why couldn't you just listen to me?"

Bobby looked at her through his eye that wasn't swollen. "You're a nurse?"

"Almost a nurse, I have a couple of more months before I get my license." She replied putting her bag down and pulling out latex gloves, a rag and an alcohol bottle.

"That's sexy. Can you go get an outfit and wear it while you check on me?" He asked with a weak chuckle.

"Shut up or I'll kick your ass." She joked pulling on the gloves. She took the rag and put alcohol on it. "This is going to sting like a bitch." She warned as she put it to his face gently. He groaned. "I told you. How does your head feel?" She asked gently cleaning the blood off of his face.

"Like I got it kicked in."

"Does it feel like there are pins and needles?"

"Like a concussion? Yea I think I have one."

"So you can't fall asleep, that's good." She said and smiled, "No I'm just kidding, but since we have time, tell me about you." She said as she started stripping him.

"This is weird. I don't know if I'm strong enough for sex yet."

"Shut up. I need to check your body out." She didn't need him to be totally naked, but she loved the way his body looked.

"You saw it last night." He said trying to laugh, but could only cough violently.

She ignored him and took out her stethoscope and blew on it. She slowly helped him turn to his side and put the stethoscope to it. "Take a deep breath." He did. "Good, now let it out." He did. She did the process a few more times before she proclaimed, "Lungs sound good. Do you have ice?"

"Look in my freezer, but I don't think so." She sat him up and put a pillow behind his head.

She went into the freezer and found nothing except a pack of frozen vegetables. She needed four icepacks.

"Hey do you think one of you guys could run to the store?" She asked.

Kerry said, "I'll call Jack he should be back soon, it might be quicker."

"Ok, tell him I need four ice packs and a bottle of Ibuprofen. Thank you." She replied grabbing the pack of frozen vegetables for his eye. She walked back into the room and threw it to him. "Put that on your eye." She pulled out her pen flashlight. "Don't blink." She shone it into his good eye real quick and watched his pupil constrict and go back to normal. "Do you have any amnesia?" He shook his head slowly. "Good. The good news is all your not going to die, but the bad news is you can't leave this bed for at least a week. Also I need to put a couple of butterfly stitches on your brow and you'll most likely have a nice scar. I hope you have sick days, because I can take off the rest of the semester and still graduate and I'm not letting you leave this bed. Also you can't smoke." The last had nothing to do with his injuries, but she didn't like the smell.

"What! I need to smoke."

"Ok, I mean your lung might collapse but go ahead." She said confidently trying to look the part.

"Fine," He said folding his arms like a kid who couldn't get his way, but flinched away from the pain, "how long do I need to stay awake?"

"I'm not a doctor, but I want you to stay awake for at least six hours. After you fall asleep, I'll wake you up every hour to make sure nothing changes."

"You need sleep too, you look like a mess." He said wishing immediately he hadn't.

She just laughed. "I'm going to say that you said that because you're concussed. I've been worried sick about *you*, asshole. I'll be right back." She got up and walked into the living room. Everyone looked up at her and it made her feel like a doctor in a waiting room full of the patient's family awaiting news of the surgery.

"How is he doc?" Nick asked not trying to be smart, but genuinely nervous.

She sighed. "First of all, I'm not a doctor. He suffered a concussion and a few bruised ribs. He has one major cut on his eyebrow and some minor ones on his nose and cheeks. He just needs rest and to be pampered by me." She paused then looked at each of the guys in turn and said. "Thank you for saving his life. Did you get a hold of Jack?"

Kerry looked up. "Yea, he should be here any minute." Just as she said that the buzzer went off.

"I'll go down and get him." Stacey said opening the door. She needed to apologize to him. When she got to the front he was with Anna. "Hey sis can you bring the stuff in, I need to talk to Jack."

She tossed the cigarette she was smoking and grabbed the White Hen Pantry bags from Jack. When she was gone Jack looked as if he was going to cry. "It's my fault. I was going to go earlier, but I needed to have a stupid meeting of how it was going to go down."

Stacey took a deep breath. "If it wasn't for you he *would* be dead. I want to apologize for earlier. He only has a concussion, a few bruised ribs and a few cuts so he'll be ok." She looked him in the eyes. "Really, it's because of you guys."

He gave her a weak smile. "Is there anything else you need?"

"I need everyone to say their goodbyes. He'll be fine, but it's getting late. I'm just going to keep him up for a few hours. Be ready to take over in case I get tired, but I should be fine. Everyone can leave. My next class isn't until Wednesday. Today is Saturday, well technically Sunday?" He nodded. "Ok. Yea just get everyone out. I'm talking in circles, I'm sorry."

He smiled. "Let's get everyone out. I need to see him first."

They walked in and Stacey put the blankets over Bobby to cover his naked body before letting Jack in. "I'll be out here." She said and walked out.

"So I was thinking Bean Street Hooligans is kinda gay. How about Mean Street Hooligans?" Jack asked when Stacey wasn't there. He would show no emotion in front of his cousin.

"You're a fucking clown." Bobby paused. "Thanks man. I mean,"

Jack put his hand up. "If our roles were switched you would have been there ten minutes earlier, well, actually you would have locked me in my room and went yourself, but whatever. Hey listen, I'm gonna get everyone out. I know how you feel about girls, but give this one a chance. She was real upset with me for letting you get stomped. If nothing else, do it for me. Who knows she could be your future ex wife." They both laughed and rapped fists. Jack opened the door and said "Victory party at my house so let's get the fuck out!" Everyone stuck their heads in the door and said bye to Bobby.

When they were all gone he heard the bolt to the front door slide home. Then Stacey walked in and put an ace bandage around his midsection before putting ice packs on each of his bruises then put another roll of ace bandage around them.

"Keep the vegetables on your eye." She called over her shoulder as she walked to the kitchen to grab a chair. She put it next to his bed and sat down. "I'm getting answers from you right now." She told him.

"Like what?" He replied.

"Where are you from?"

"Somerville."

"What street in Somerville?"

He hesitated. "Hinckley St. Look if you want to know my past, you have to know that I am a different person now."

"I don't care who you were. I just want to know the basics."

He sighed. "My name is Bobby Cross. My parents are dead and I work for an airline company. I smoke, I drink and I fight. I don't trust women, but I am willing to give you a chance, because my cousin thinks you're worth it and he is a lot smarter than I am. I'm twenty four years old and have a used 2001 Nissan Maxima. I live here and only got this apartment because Jack's mother co signed with me. I believe in God but don't go to church and I never went to college. I got in my first fight before I can remember and had my first drink the same night I lost my virginity when I was thirteen. I probably corrupted my cousin and I'm over protective of him and my friends. I played high school football and I hate people who think they are better than me. Is there anything else you want to know?" He replied a little more irritated then he wanted to sound.

"I didn't mean to make you upset." She said quite taken aback. "What do you want to know about me?" She asked trying to salvage the conversation.

"I don't want to know anything about you. Not now anyway, we will have time for that, if you want to get to know me better, that is."

She was thrown off by his sudden casualness. She had heard a few stories about him at the bar. He was some badass who threw fists every chance he got and didn't trust women enough to date them, but she had no fear of him. To her he was a misunderstood sweetheart. She would try her hardest to break him.

She set the alarm for six hours and started feeling the long day in her bones. She asked, "Do you have coffee?"

"Yea, look I didn't mean," He started trying to find the words he could use, but nothing came.

She smiled and said, "When that alarm goes off you can go to sleep."

Bobby woke up the next day stiff and sore, worse than he had ever been in his whole life. If she had woken him up at all through the night, he didn't remember. He didn't even remember falling asleep in the first place.

He looked over at Stacey, who was still awake. She was watching Boy meets world and didn't know he was watching her. Her head kept falling towards her chest and immediately snapping back up. Bobby watched amused.

"Excuse me, nurse? I think my pillow can be fluffed." He smiled at her and she smiled back.

"Glad to see you made it through the night." She got up and walked around the bed to get a better look at his eye. The swelling was down a little. She took the ace bandage off and took the ice packs and put them in the freezer with the vegetables and got a glass of water so he could take more Ibuprofen. "How's your breathing, any problems?"

"No, now come lie down and get some sleep. It's my turn to take care of you." He said and she hesitated. "Lay down or I'm going outside and running until I collapse." He threatened.

She stripped down to her underwear and pulled the same kind of T-shirt Anna had the night before, out of his closet. She lay down, but didn't want to get too close. Bobby pulled her close and even though it hurt like a bitch he made no noise.

"I swear to God if I hurt you I'm getting up." She said seeing through his mask of toughness.

"Go to sleep." He said kissing her forehead and before he pulled his lips away she was out cold.

He waited impatiently for an hour before he dared to get out of bed. He wrote a note telling her that if she woke up that he just went to the store and would be right back. She would be mad as hell, but he didn't care.

He took his phone out and seen a text from Jack. *I need to talk to you right now text me when you get this.* He wondered what it was about but texted back *I'll be over there in fifteen minutes.* He snuck back into his room and found jeans and a T-shirt and put them on making sure Stacey didn't move.

When he got outside the first thing he did was light a cigarette. He inhaled as deep as he could and let it out slow. Ah the addiction of nicotine. He jumped in his Maxima and took of for Jack's house.

It was a warm, beautiful day, so he rolled his windows down and slipped in his Talib Kweli CD. As he was waiting at the red light at the entrance of Medford SQ. he glanced at the TV store window and seen the soccer field from last night. There was a guy pointing from the parking lot to the field and back. Underneath it said, "Has hooliganism finally made it across the pond?" He didn't know what to think. Finally a horn blast from behind him broke his trance and so he pulled away.

As he drove towards Jack's he started to get paranoid. Everyone he passed was peering in at his soul. Everyone was judging him. He was so entranced by this that he almost hit a cop.

He pulled over, got out of his car and leaned against it trying to collect his thoughts and compose himself. He took one final drag of his forgotten cigarette and flicked it away. Suddenly the air around him didn't feel right. Something was about to go wrong and he didn't know what, but he didn't like it.

He knocked on Jack's door and Anna answered it in Jack's shirt. "Doesn't anybody have school anymore?" He asked. He was angry that she was there and he didn't know why.

"It's Sunday asshole. Doesn't anybody have work anymore?" She retorted.

"Touché, I banged out on my nurse's orders." He flashed a quick smile trying to lighten the mood.

Jack was sitting at his kitchen table with his cell phone open in front of him. "Have you watched the news?" He asked as Bobby pulled up a chair. "There was a guy fishing on the beach who recognized you and now you're a suspect in these brutal beatings." He put these last words in air quotes.

"What the fuck ever happened to not ratting? Does that mean I gotta go turn myself in?" Bobby asked getting nervous.

"Well watch the news clip, I put it on my Tivo." Jack replied starting off towards his room.

The news clip basically said that two groups of people fought at the soccer field behind Kmart, but what got Bobby's attention was the man they interviewed.

Apparently the guy on the beach was fishing when he heard a commotion. When he looked back, he saw a bunch of guys kicking another guy on the ground. Bobby couldn't stop thinking how retarded Bostonians sounded while getting interviewed with their accent. The man on the TV said that's when he heard a Minutemen suck chant, so he looked towards the sound and saw four guys running towards the field. Then they fought the other guys who were kicking the other guy. What a fucking retard, Bobby thought. He said it reminded him of soccer hooligans he once saw on TV. The guy stopped and actually put a finger to his chin. Bobby didn't think anyone actually did that stupid shit. Then the guy said, "Come to think of it they were hooligans, right? I mean they were actually real life

Boston Fighting Cox hooligans." The guy chuckled and the camera went back to studio and Bobby shut it off.

"That wasn't the whole thing. The anchor said how the cops were looking for you to question. He said the guy knew who you were and called the police." Jack said from behind him, leaning against the door jam.

"So, I mean, what the fuck should I do? Do I go to the cops or call them?" He let out a long sigh and lit a cigarette. Normally Jack would have freaked out, but under the circumstances he didn't mind.

Bobby paced back and forth for ten minutes in pure agonizing silence. "I should call them." He finally said and pulled out his cell. He saw he had a text. It was a kid he used to play football with. *I want fucking in!* That was all it said and all that Bobby needed to see. He held it up for Jack to see. After all, it was Jack who wanted to start the firm. When he read it his eyes lit up.

"Holy shit Bobby, you're famous." Anna said. "You two should start a Facebook page for that. If you want to make it legit that is."

Bobby didn't like that anymore then he liked the cops looking for him. "How do I do a Facebook, I've never had one?" Jack asked. So while Anna was explaining it to Jack, Bobby decided to call the cops, because he didn't care how to use a Facebook.

The phone rang three times before a lady picked up and said in a droning, tired voice, "Somerville police department, how can I help you?"

"Hi, I understand I am wanted for questioning. I would like to turn myself in, if that's what I need to do." Bobby replied in the most pleasant voice he could muster up.

"What is your name sir?" The lady replied in an agitated voice.

"Bobby Cross. A guy fishing told the cops I was in a huge fight last night." A couple of minutes went by as he heard her typing on a keyboard.

"Ok Mr. Cross. Um, I am going to get a detective to come and talk to you hold on just one second." She said more interested now then before.

"Ok." Bobby said sounding tired. He needed to come up with a story and quick. He had a million different scenarios running through his head when there finally was a click.

"This is detective Morales." A strong confident voice came on the phone. "Is this Mr. Cross?"

"Yes."

"Ok, so as of right now I just want to ask a couple of questions. Why don't you come down to the police station as soon as possible and we can get it out of the way." He said pleasantly.

"Ok, I'll be down as soon as I can." Bobby replied and hung up. He turned to Jack. "What the fuck do I say?"

Now, as you can understand, Bobby has been in trouble with the law before, but was always let go due to lack of evidence or pure luck. This time there was a witness, as well as the bruises and cuts on his face.

"You want me to come?" Jack asked. Bobby just shook his head. He would come up with something then call jack to let him know.

"I'll call you soon." Bobby said and walked out lighting up another cigarette.

Jack gave Anna a weak smile and went to lie down in the bed. "What do you think he should say?" He asked her as she lay on top of him and rested her head on his chest. She didn't answer because she couldn't. She just leaned up to kiss his chin and put her head back on his chest.

As Bobby was driving towards the police station, he tried to come up with the perfect thing to say, but his concentration kept being broken by text messages and phone calls saying they wanted to fight with him. He knew some of the numbers, but a lot of them were unknown. He was getting aggravated with everyone. He just wanted to go back to bed.

He pulled into the police station, which of course had no parking lot for the public, but he forgot because his mind wasn't all there. He pulled back out and parked on the side street. He got out and lit another cigarette before he walked in.

"Can I help you?" the lady sitting in the glassed off reception desk asked in an annoyed voice. It was probably the same lady that he talked to on the phone, but Bobby couldn't tell.

"Yes, ma'am, I am here to speak with detective Morales please." He replied.

"Name," She asked.

"Bobby Cross." He answered.

She typed it in then he saw her eyes light up a little. It was almost as if they had never talked on the phone. For all he knew this was a different secretary.

"One moment, please." She said as she picked up the phone. "Bobby Cross is here for you, detective." She nodded and hung up the phone. "You can have a seat over there, he will be right out."

Bobby opted to stand because sitting hurt too much. He paced back and forth for only a minute or so before the detective was opening the door and calling him in. His back was holding the door open and his right hand was sticking out. Bobby shook it firmly. He looked at Bobby's face questioningly, but said nothing. He would wait until they were in the interrogation room.

There was a field of desks behind the door. To the left were four rooms for meetings or interrogations. Morales opened the door to the first one. "Take a seat" he said pointing to one of two seats on the left side of the table. He sat opposite of it. "Now, you are not being charged with anything as of right now. You can wait for a lawyer, but like I said you're not being charged, so you have nothing to worry about."

"I have nothing to hide from you, sir." Bobby replied innocently.

"Please, just call me Seth." He replied and Bobby gave him a quizzical look. "I know, my dad is Puerto Rican and my mom is Jewish. It's weird." He gave Bobby a million dollar whitened smile; all teeth were straight and seemed to sparkle.

"Yea, it kind of is, Seth." Bobby replied testing the name on the tip of his tongue.

"Let's start with this, Bobby, what were you doing at that soccer field last night?"

"Well, I'm not going to lie to you. I had a fight with a girl I was, um, being intimate with. My cousin Jack and my friend's were supposed to meet me in the parking lot for a few drinks. I was the first to arrive there so I started drinking in the field. Next thing I know I'm on the ground and these guys are kicking the shit out of me." He looked up at the cop, who was listening intently and patiently, while writing down notes here and there. "Thank God my cousin and friends showed up or I would probably be dead right now. I decided I didn't need to go to the hospital so they took me home."

He nodded, "Ok, at what point did you decide you were going to call the cops?"

"We weren't going to. As far as we were concerned the guys that jumped me got what they deserved and would get up the next morning in pain." He said making everything up on the spot.

"What about the 'Minutemen suck' chant? It kind of suggests that they knew they were Minutemen fans and that this was premeditated." Seth said.

"I know a couple of them had Minutemen hats on and that's probably why. My cousin has a real hatred for the Minutemen."

"Yea, I bet." He replied flashing his pearly whites again, "Well, from your story, if it checks out that is, you have nothing to worry about. But if these guys decide to press charges, then your friends are in trouble. I am going to follow up with these guys in the hospital. I'll give you a call when I am done there."

"But, they were just sticking up for me; wouldn't it be the other way around? Shouldn't I be the one who presses charges? I mean, I don't want to. I am just trying to figure this all out."

"Relax. Nothing is definite; I am just giving you different scenarios."

Bobby scratched his head and nodded. "Ok. So should I tell my cousin and my friends to come see you?"

"Well let's see what happens with their stories first. Can I have a number to reach you at?" When Bobby finished giving him his number, Seth Morales stood. "To be honest with you, and I shouldn't say this, but the only reason your friends can get in trouble is because they used weapons and an eye witness saw it. Now, like I said, you're not being charged with anything so you are free to go and I will call you when I get out of the hospital to let you know what will happen."

He led Bobby back out to the lobby. Bobby stuck out his hand and Seth took it. "Thank you for not being a dickhead Seth. Sorry, but a lot of lawmen are dicks it's just nice to see one who isn't."

Seth smiled. "Thank you for coming in. It looks good on your part."

Bobby left the police station and started jogging towards his car, but in all his haste he had forgotten about his pain. He keeled over and vomited in the middle of the street. "Fuck me." He muttered and continued to his car at a slow walking pace. He dialed Jack, who picked up on the first ring. "Get everyone over to your house right now." He hung up and sped off to Jack's.

By the time Bobby got there everyone was sitting around Jack's table. To Bobby it looked like a scene out of a King Arthur movie or something like King Arthur and the Knights of the Round Table. He chuckled aloud.

"Calls us here and laughs at us." Nick said.

"Sorry," He replied, "first off since I left here earlier I have received like fifty texts and calls from people saying they want to join our firm. Ok A. I don't know what the fuck that means and B. who the fuck is giving out my fucking number?"

"Bobby, what happened at the police station? None of us are giving out your number, so let's talk about the cops." Jack said getting straight to the point.

"Fine, but let's note that I am fucking heated ok? So I talked to the cop and this is how last night went down."

He told them all the detailed description he came up with of what happened and what was going to happen. He looked at each of them and asked if they were in or if he should say he had been mistaken and that it must have been other people who had helped him.

Anna stepped out of the bathroom with a towel around her head as Bobby was finishing his story. He didn't hear the shower running because his mind was going in circles.

"Holy shit you scared the fuck out of me." He said jumping.

"Sorry I couldn't help overhearing, but you guys just had your first meeting as a firm." She said smiling.

"Anna, here, took the liberty of putting us on this Facebook thing. We've already got 150 hits." Jack said happily. "They're not just from Boston either. They're from all over the US!"

Bobby looked at Jack then shook his head. "I'm going home before Stacey knows I left and yells at me."

"It's a little too late for that!" A voice yelled from Jack's room.

"Jack, who the fuck was that," He asked through clenched teeth.

He chuckled guiltily. "Well you said to call *everyone.*"

He mouthed the words I'm going to fucking kill you right as Stacey emerged from Jack's room with Kerry and Lisa. "Stacey." Bobby said changing his scowl into a wide grin.

"I told you that you needed rest!"

"Well I had to go to the police station."

"We're going home, now." She demanded. She wasn't trying to be the boss of him, just trying to make sure he was ok. She realized how she must have sounded to them and gave a crooked smile.

"Yes ma'am." Bobby said realizing she was being playful. "I'll call you guys when Seth calls me. He's the detective, a real nice guy."

When they walked into the apartment Stacey said, "Lie down. Would you like something to eat?"

"No *you* lie down. You must be exhausted. Do *you* want something to eat?" he retorted.

"No I'm ok you're the one who is injured."

"I'm just going to jump in the shower. I'll be right in to cuddle. That's what I really need."

"I would ask if you need company but I'd probably fall asleep in there. Ok I'm gonna lie down." She opened the bedroom door and paused. "Promise me you'll be right in."

"Of course my dear, I promise." He said with a sardonic smile. In all the years since his parents died, he never in a million years thought he'd play house, but here he was bread and buttered into what everyone thought to be the American dream.

She just gave him a look and walked into the bedroom. He turned on the shower and jumped in. he wasn't going to, but he figured it might make him feel better. He didn't realize how bad the water against his cuts and bruises would hurt. Tears stung the corners of his eyes and he thought better of soaping up.

When he got out his phone started ringing. He picked it up after the first ring. "Hello?"

"May I speak to Mr. Cross?"

"Speaking,"

"It's Seth. I am at the hospital right now. Good news, they aren't pressing charges and said it was mistaken identity. I'm confident that none of you are going to tell me the truth, but that's where we are right now."

"Thank you Seth. Any other questions please call."

"Don't worry, I will. Have a nice day."

After they hung up Bobby called Jack to let him know.

After Jack hung up with Bobby he walked back into his kitchen to let everyone know. They were all huddled around his computer staring at the Facebook page. They were getting constant hits. People from everywhere were commenting and sending messages saying they were in. The Fighting Cox were going to play the Baltimore Oracles in a couple of days so they had Anna post the comment that anyone who was in the Baltimore area and wanted to set up a meet to message the creator of the page.

It took five minutes but they got ten people who answered. Anna then sent a message to all ten people telling them that they had to get together and figure it out. Once everyone agreed on a bar to meet up at, they would figure out a major and get back to them. They agreed to come up to Boston, reluctant at first, but coming around to the idea in the end.

"Wow. Is this shit is really happening?" Jack asked dumbfounded. "We've created a firm."

Anna gave him a kiss. "Good job baby, even though I hate the idea I'm happy you stuck to it," She looked at her watch, "Oh shit I got a study group, can someone give me a ride?"

"Do you really have to go?" Jack asked sounding upset.

"Yea, but I'll be back later." She replied in her innocent voice.

"Yea I have to go too," Lisa said throwing her arms up in a shrug, "Got to make up a Physics test what are ya gonna do?"

"I'll take them." Ronnie volunteered.

When they were gone, Jack turned to Nick and Jason. "Our bar is obviously Razzy's right?" After they nodded he got on his phone and called his cousin.

"What's up?" Bobby whispered into the phone. He didn't want to wake Stacey up.

"Friday,"

"What the fuck are you talking about man?"

"We set up a fight."

"I don't even know if I'll be alright by then." Bobby replied.

"It's ok man. We'll figure that out then. Meantime call all those people back and tell them to meet us at Razzy's tonight.

"You got it boss." Bobby replied and Jack liked the sound of it.

He sat there quietly and played around with the word in his mind. Boss, his cousin just called him boss. In all the years he could remember, he had never felt superior to Bobby until now. Now he was the boss, he was the one everyone would look upon when in need.

"You alright, Jack?" Nick asked breaking him out of his day dream.

"Yea, fine," He replied and his lips turned up into a satanic smile.

8

They all gathered in the back room, thanks to Nancy it was closed off for the night. She had also set up the mic and speakers for them. Beers weren't on the house tonight, but they were half priced for everyone in the back room.

There were twenty people who showed up. Of the twenty only eleven were new. So they would show up at the first fight with fifteen fighters, Bobby was still doubtful as to whether he could fight. It wasn't such a bad turnout, considering in the movie they had less people and still tore shit up all across England, but that was also a movie and it made Bobby feel a little queasy knowing his cousin wasn't able to separate reality from a movie. He was living in a fantasy world playing a game with everyone's life in this room.

"This shits really happening, bro." Ronnie was saying into Bobby's ear. He just shook his head and went outside for a smoke.

"We're about to start, where the fuck is he going?" Jack asked.

"I don't know, man, but I known him for awhile now. Never have I seen him act like this. It's like," Ronnie paused trying to put a finger on what he was really trying to say here, "He's going soft."

"I know what you mean." Jack said a little distraught.

Nick walked over to them and said, "These guys went to our high school?"

"Yea, various years though. I think maybe one or two graduated with us." Jack replied looking out at the motley crew sitting before them waiting anxiously. He grabbed the mic and stuttered out, "We're going to start just as soon as Bobby gets back." This was followed by loud applause to the sound of Bobby's name and Jack gritted his teeth a little.

Bobby was leaning with his back to the wall and had one leg up against it taking deep inhales of smoke when Nancy came out.

"What's wrong sweetheart?" She asked lighting her own cigarette.

Bobby smiled weakly trying to mask his worries. "Nothing, it's just my crazy cousin." She looked at him like he was crazy. He put his hand up, "I know, I know. I shouldn't be the one saying that considering my past, but I mean he's taking this shit too far. It was different when it was just me fighting, but c'mon there's a bunch of people in there who are going into a fight which none of us know the enemy. I never in my life had fought someone I didn't know how well they fought."

"Bullshit, Bobby, how many nights did I have to call the cops on you because you were drunk and trying to start a fight with my other customers? You, Jack, Ronnie, Nick and

Jason are like sons to me, so let's be honest ok?" She looked lovingly at him and put her hand on his wrist. "I don't know what's going on in that crazy head of yours, but I know it's not about all those guys back there. What's really going on Bobby?"

He sighed and put his head against the wall. "Look what happened to me Nancy. I have been fighting my whole life and look what happened!" He shouted on the brink of tears. "Jack," he paused swallowing back those tears. He started again almost whispering, "Jack is the only family who hasn't shunned me, probably the only person I can say I truly love. What if he gets in trouble and I can't help him?" He looked at her like he was lost and she was his savior.

She put a hand on his shoulder, "You put too much burden on yourself Bobby. I don't mean to sound like a bitch right now, but you are not that man's father. He will do what he wants, when he wants and not you or anyone else, for that matter, *can* stop him. What're you going to handcuff him in his basement?" He looked away breaking her accusing stare. She was right of course, but he didn't want to hear it. "If you really want to help him, get back there and support him. Be his right hand man."

"I know you're right, Nancy, but that don't mean I have to accept it." He said tossing his cigarette and walking back in.

He walked back through the crowded bar catching accidental elbows, which was just adding to his irritation, not to mention almost putting him on his knees in pain. He finally made it through the bulk of the crowd and was walking towards the back when someone grabbed the back of his shirt; causing him to fall back a little and making his injuries flare up in pain again. He turned around to see Jackie G.

"C'mon man not here." He said just tired and in pain.

"God damn if we didn't fuck you up boy. Don't worry I'm not here for a fight. On the contrary, I am here to accept your cousin's offer. I will start the firm for the Minutemen," He extended his hand, "No hard feelings?"

"No." Bobby replied cautiously grabbing for his ribs and taking Jackie's callused hand in his own. His lips curled into a sickly smile as he tightened his grip and shook. "No hard feelings at all."

Jackie G turned and walked out weaving his way through the crowd. Bobby watched until Jackie was outside before he walked to the back.

He could see everyone was getting drunk. Jack was nervously playing with his hands. He nodded to him to start. Jack walked back to the mic and picked it up with shaky hands. It looked like his nerves were getting the better of him.

"Alright everyone, let's get started. Thank you for coming and supporting us. I would like to start by telling you guys the rules." He held up his hand and stuck up one finger. "Rule number one. This stays here in this room. Do not under any circumstances tell anyone about what goes on here. If we want to recruit more people, that is between me and Bobby. Number two, do not rat, ever. Number three, never ever run from a fight, no matter how many people we are outnumbered by. Number four, if you are hurt or injured, lie about how you got hurt or injured to outsiders. Number five, and probably the most important, never ever let anyone fight alone." He looked towards Bobby, who nodded. "If you break any of these rules, you will be kicked out and I will personally kick seven shades of shit out of you," He chuckled inwardly at the reference to the movie, "If you do not agree with anything I am saying then leave now, there's the door." No one moved so he continued.

"I am going off of what I saw in the movie *Green Street Hooligans.* We will modify things as we go along but as of right now, I am your major and Bobby is my right hand man." He saw the look Anna was giving him, but ignored it. "Razzy's will be our bar since Nancy is nice enough to allow us here. We have gotten in contact with a rep from Baltimore's firm and we have set up a meet on Friday. We'll start drinking here and make our way to somewhere in Boston, near Fenway. Now this is new to all of us so feedback is also appreciated. I think that's it for now if there are any questions come up to me, Bobby, Nick, Jason or Ronnie and ask."

Bobby thought he did an alright job. He took a swig of his Bud Light as Jack clapped him on the back making him spit it back up onto the bar.

"How was it?" He asked with a certain hint of glee in his voice.

Bobby was wiping his face so Stacey said, "Not bad, but boy is Anna going to be pissed."

"Yup, you just dug yourself a hole my man." Bobby said knowing what he promised her from Stacey.

"Nah, she'll come around." Jack replied not entirely believing himself.

"Yea, Jack? Where'd she go then?" Bobby snickered scanning the room. Anna was nowhere to be found.

Jack ran down to the other bar room where he asked Ruth, who was behind the bar, if she saw Anna.

"I'm sorry, Jack, I'm so busy I can't see anyone." That was when someone grabbed his ass. He turned around to see a random girl smiling.

"Please, not now." He begged the attractive girl who was visibly swaying.

"What's the matter? Am I not hot enough for you?" She slurred back. She put her hands on his chest and slid them down. All of sudden, with lightning fast speed, her head snapped back and slammed off of the bar.

"Don't worry Jack. I won't tell my sister." Stacey said brushing passed him and walking outside. Jack looked around, but no one was looking at the knocked out girl on the floor gushing blood.

"Hey, um, Ruth!" He yelled out to Ruth, who put two shots in front of a customer before she raced over. "Yeah, so this girl was talking to me and I guess she passed out, I tried to catch her, but it was too late."

"Oh Jesus, did she hit her face?" she asked. She couldn't see over the bar.

"Yea, she hit it right off of the bar. I think her nose is broke." He replied and walked outside to find Anna.

She was talking to Stacey when he walked up. She took a haul of her cigarette and looked at him. "I know we only been dating for, like, a couple of days, but you already lied to me. I'm not going to go crazy, but I am worried. Do not try to take that away from me. Let me finish my smoke and I'll be back in."

He stopped in his tracks, thought a second, then turned around and went back in, confused about what had just happened.

Bobby was talking to Nick when Jack walked in. Nick was jabbing in the air while Bobby was howling with laughter and holding his side.

Jack walked up to the bar and ordered four shots of Jack. Nancy gave him a look, but fulfilled his order. She lined them up in front of him and he snapped back all four without so much as a grimace.

"Hi, Jack, my name is Mike. I just had a question." Jack turned around to a guy who was at least 6'7" and looked like he was on steroids.

Jack stuck out his hand and shook Mike's vice like grip. "What's going on Mike?"

"Well in that movie the called themselves GSE, what are we going to call ourselves?" Mike asked folding his massive arms over his huge barreled chest.

"Jesus Chrlst you're fucking big. Sorry, I didn't mean to be rude." Jack replied before he could hold his tongue. Mike just let out a big hearty laugh. "Um, I was thinking about Bean Street Hooligans?"

"I don't like it. It sounds too much like the movie." Jason was saying as he walked over from the jukebox.

"I agree and it also sounds like a two year old made it up." Mike said.

"Ok, well what do you guys suggest?" Jack replied maybe a little too defensively.

"How bout you just call yourselves FCN?" Nancy asked from across the bar after no one answered.

"What's FCN?" The three of them asked in unison.

"Fighting Cox Nation," She replied smiling.

"Wow. I like that, a lot actually," Jack said, "How about you guys?"

"I like it too." Mike said

"Yea, wow Nance you're a genius." Jason chimed in.

Jack walked up to the mic and made the announcement over the speakers about their new name. They all went berserk. Ronnie started chanting, "FCN, FCN, FCN" and pretty soon the whole bar, even the people in the public side of it, were chanting.

9

Friday was game day, which meant it would be the first brawl for the FCN. Bobby had to be in work at four AM. It would be his first day back since he was jumped, but he felt a little better and knew that he could ask his supervisors to give him a job that wouldn't require much physical labor. He would work until 12:30 in the afternoon, so he figured he would get a nice nap in before the game.

He stepped out onto his stoop and stopped for a minute. It wasn't cold, but it wasn't warm either. It felt quaint. He had a feeling, but couldn't tell you what it was. It was a foreign thing he had never felt.

He lit a cigarette and put it to his lips as it occurred to him what the feeling was, his nerves. He had never been nervous about a fight, not one he could remember anyway. He didn't like the butterflies that were doing loop de loops in his stomach.

He looked out at the quiet street getting ready to be full of traffic in a few hours and then back at his building. He knew he shouldn't be fighting tonight, in fact shouldn't even be on his way to work, but he wouldn't leave his cousin no matter what the consequences were. He nodded inwardly to himself and walked to his car. He had just made a secret pact with himself to protect his cousin no matter the cost. Whether the cost was his life or another man's, no one would harm Jack.

"Yea, no one not even God himself will harm him as long as I'm around." He said aloud to the desolate street.

As he drove past the state police barracks in Wellington Circle, he couldn't help but play the same scenario in his head that haunted his dreams the night before:

The rain hurts as it pelts Bobby in the face. He is standing beside Jack like a loyal pit bull ready to attack at its master's command. The FCN is lined up in a straight line. Facing them about 100 ft away are their enemies, the Briscoe Street Bullies (or BSB) ready and waiting for someone to make the first move.

Bobby's breath is seen but he doesn't feel cold, he knows his body is still bruised, but feels no pain. He knows something will happen to Jack, but he cannot speak to warn him.

His breathing deepens, becomes longer exhales and all of a sudden his breath fills the field like a huge cloak of fog and now he can no longer see.

He hears Jack scream, "Bobby!" and his fear sets in as he cannot see where to go. He cannot help the only person he cares about.

He gets on his knees and crawls, thinking he would be able to see better from the ground. He tries to scream out Jack's name, but the only thing that comes is more fog-like breath. He lays his head on the ground and closes his eyes.

He comes to at Jack's table and is surrounded by Anna, Jack's mother and father, Ronnie, Nick and Jason.

Anna speaks up first. "You should have taken care of him," And it feels like a stake goes through his heart.

"What are you talking about?" He shot back at her.

"He was my baby!" Jack's mother screamed and another stake hit his heart.

"How could you do that to him?" Ronnie, Nick, Jason and Jack's father almost sing together in one monotonous tone.

Bobby just looks from one person to another and back. Nick got up and punched him in the face and Bobby blacked out.

He woke back up in a dark confined area. The smell was nauseating and whatever he was laying on felt alive. "How could you kill me?" Jack whispered into Bobby's ear and he felt maggots crawling around Jack's body.

All at once it hit him like a brick. He was lying on top of Jack in his casket. He vomited all over and squirmed trying to get out, but to no avail. He was constricted to this space for all eternity, a punishment suited for the crime of not protecting Jack.

He remembered waking in a cold sweat, the blankets so wet that he thought he'd pissed the bed. He looked over and Stacey was staring at him with shocked horror, "What the hell did you just dream about?" She had asked.

"Nothing," He paused seeing that she was scared for him, "I can't remember."

He could have been sitting at that light in front of the State Police barracks forever if not for the trucker's horn that made him come to from his thoughts. He shivered and waved behind him before he took off.

His phone started going off, causing him to jump a little. He picked it up without checking the caller id, "Hello?"

"So you went to work?" Stacey asked.

"Yea," Bobby replied with a nervous giggle, "I was feeling better."

"I don't understand why you won't listen to me Bobby!" She yelled and hung up.

"Because you're not my mother," He replied into the dial tone.

Jack woke up later, around 11 AM, unlike Bobby he didn't care too much about his job ever since Anna and the FCN came into his life. He just laid in bed thinking about the amazing four days of make up sex he'd had with Anna.

It was the same routine, wake up, sex, shower, sex, breakfast, sex, she'd go to school for a few hours and then come back, sex, lunch, sex, TV, sex, dinner, sex and then sleep.

He got up and stretched as he walked over to his computer when Nick walked in. "What's the word boss?" He asked.

"Nothing, just trying to find out where the fuck this fight should happen. I can't find shit anywhere man." Jack said without too much enthusiasm.

"You should ask Ronnie. He's always making deliveries around Fenway." Nick said putting his jacket over one of the chairs.

"Where is Ronnie?" Jack asked puzzled.

"I was helping him with his deliveries, you know, to make a little extra cash and then Lisa and Kerry called him, cause they wanted to hang out. They said they couldn't listen to Anna and Stacey bitch anymore. Anna went to class, but Stacey didn't have school and Bobby went to work so she went back home to get more clothes and to hang out with them." Nick said as delicately as he could so that Jack didn't get mad at him.

"Oh and what would they be bitching about?" Jack asked.

"Well Anna is upset about you being the major, and Stacey is pissed that Bobby's gonna fight."

"Well Anna wanted to fuck that guy in the movie, so what's the difference? And Bobby isn't gonna fight."

"Dude, c'mon, that was a movie, she doesn't really want you to fight and do you really think Bobby is gonna let you go in alone?"

"Well she said what Bobby did to that kid at Fenway was hot and I don't need Bobby's fucking protection." Jack said getting irritated. He loved Bobby, but couldn't stand when he tried to step in to play the father roll like Jack was his son. He just couldn't take it anymore.

"I'm gonna be real honest with you here so don't get mad. If Anna wanted a fighter she would've fucked Bobby that night instead of you. I don't know what your problem with your cousin is, but all he's trying to do is watch your back like any one of us would. I don't understand why you try to compete with him, but it's got to stop." It was like a slap in the face to Jack.

"Yea, well I have no intention of getting into a pissing contest with Bobby. You may be right about Anna, but it's too late now." Jack replied coldly as he sat down at his table.

"No it's not. You can give it to Bobby. He'll do it, no problem; you think he likes Stacey enough to say no? It's Bobby for Christ's sake." Nick said chuckling.

"I want it though. This is my project not his." Jack said backing himself into a corner.

"So then he's your right hand man and you can't get mad at him for getting your back like that." Nick replied wishing he had never brought the subject up.

Nick sat down at the table with Jack to wait for Ronnie to come. Neither of them spoke a word to each other while waiting. They also never spoke of the conversation they had that day again. Maybe Jack was a little jealous of Bobby and maybe he wasn't. Either way it was a secret between the two friends that would stay buried between them.

Bobby left the airport like he always did exhausted and pissed off. People had known what happened to him; of course they did, because working at the airport was like fucking high school all over. Everyone one knew each other's business, but they didn't know the whole story, which was bad because it left people to speculate and start rumors. According to the latest story going around work, he killed someone and threw them into the Mystic river that night.

He had talked to Jason who was now over Jack's with Ronnie, Nick and the girls. They agreed to meet up at Razzy's for a few drinks before the game. The game started at 7:10 PM so they would meet at the bar around 5 PM. They didn't have tickets so they would watch the game at a bar near Fenway and then meet up with the BSB after.

When he got to his apartment Stacey was sitting on his couch. She had gone there from Jack's after Bobby called Jason. She looked at him nervously and said, "I don't think you should fight tonight Bobby."

"I will if I see someone needs me. Shouldn't you be at school?" He asked taking his sweatshirt off slowly. He was feeling better, but the slightest jerk caused his pain to flare back up.

"No, I had today off. Bobby your ribs are not healed yet! You will be useless and will get hurt more!" She said uncrossing her legs and getting up and walking towards him. "You shouldn't have even worked today."

"I like how you try to control me. Stacey, I tried to tell you before, no one can control me. I will do what I want and not you or anyone else will tell me otherwise." He said coldly walking into his room.

"I know that. I just want you to know that you could get really hurt." She said following him. "And I know that I'm not your mother or your girlfriend, even, but I really like you and am only looking out for your best interests." When he said nothing, she sighed and said, "Please just take what I said into consideration."

"I like what we have. Maybe we could become more, but for now just," He stopped trying to figure out the right words, "Just let me be who I am." He pulled his covers down getting into bed only wearing his boxer briefs. "Right now I need to take a nap, so are you interested in joining?" He asked holding the covers up for her to get in. She did, but while Bobby started to softly snore, she laid awake thinking about him and how things would happen tonight. She really cared for him and didn't want him hurt, but it was clear that he wouldn't listen to her and it worried her, a lot.

Bobby woke up at 4:30 to his phone ringing. It was Jack telling him to meet at his house and not Razzy's.

He started getting ready as Stacey slowly rose. She fell asleep after an hour of worrying and didn't want to move yet. Bobby looked at her, wanting to apologize, but in the end said nothing and just went to Jack's with Stacey.

"What's going on guys?" Bobby asked as he walked into Jack's house. Jack, Nick and Ronnie were all huddled around Jack's computer. Lisa and Kerry were in Jack's room watching TV.

"We can't fucking figure out where this will all go down." Nick said.

"Yea I even considered the fucking Hatch Shell." Jack added.

"Where they have the concerts?" Bobby asked.

"Yea, but it's like a forty minute walk from Fenway. There is no way I'm walking that far when I'm drunk." Jack said never taking his eyes off of the computer screen.

Bobby thought a second and said, "What about the train tracks?"

Jack looked up. "That's not a bad idea at all."

"Yea, I could go snip the fence before the game starts over near Jillian's. The cops shouldn't be down there. We would have to figure out the train schedule, but I think we could pull this off." Bobby said proudly.

"Ok, I'll give John a call and let him know." Jack said flipping his phone open.

"Who the fuck is John?" Ronnie asked.

"He's the BSB major. We've been communicating through email so I just gave him my number." Jack replied putting his phone to his ear.

"How are you doing ladies?" Bobby waved into the bedroom and they waved back. Stacey silently brushed passed Bobby and went into Jack's room to watch TV with them.

"I need to talk to you Bobby," Ronnie said grabbing Bobby's arm.

"So talk,"

"Not here. You think you need a smoke?" Ronnie said hinting at going outside. Bobby followed him willingly enough.

He lit his cigarette and asked, "What's up?"

"We don't want you to fight tonight." He said hesitantly.

"What the fuck you mean." Bobby said getting angry.

"We want you to go home and rest man. We don't want you to get hurt."

"Stop talking. I'm going and none of you will stop me. I won't leave you guys open." He threw his cigarette and walked to his car. "I'll see you at Razzy's." He called out behind him. Other than Jack, Ronnie was his best friend. They came up together on Hinckley St. and so Ronnie saying that just hit him deep and upset him more. It started to look like the world was against him.

They all walked into Razzy's together and Ruth directed them to the back. When they got back there most of the FCN were already there waiting. Jack walked to the bar and bought Anna and him a drink. "Have you seen Bobby?" He asked.

"Not yet sweetheart." Nancy replied gloomily.

Jack took a sip of his Jack and Coke and asked Ronnie, "How pissed was he?"

"I don't want to see him tonight, that's how pissed." He replied looking around nervously.

Bobby walked in as Jack was shooting the shit with the rest of "The Nation". He ignored everyone who tried to say hi and went straight to Jack.

"I don't give a fuck how fucking hurt I am, I will *not* let you go in alone do you understand me?" He said furiously jabbing him in the chest with his finger.

"Bobby, you have to understand, it's for your own health." Jack almost whispered.

"I don't give a fuck!" He snapped back not trying to keep his voice down. All heads turned to the two cousins.

"Alright, but please hang back until you see someone that needs help." He replied giving up. No one would stop Bobby and he understood.

"Ok, that sounds agreeable. By the way, it's done." He whispered into Jack's ear.

"What is?" He asked looking confused.

Bobby looked at his watch, "Where are they drinking?" He asked.

"Um, John told me they were going to check out the House of Blues, why?"

"Ok. Get on the phone with him tell him after the game walk out of the House of Blues and turn left," Bobby said visualizing the walk from the House of Blues, "Walk down and take a left on Ipswich St. Follow that until he sees a bridge. When he gets under the bridge, while making sure no one sees him, look to the left. There will be a hole in the fence leading to the tracks. Once they're on the tracks turn left and start walking we will be a little ways down."

Jack was amazed he had figured out an entire plan in only a couple of hours. Jack had been trying to figure it out for more than a day.

He finished his drink and looked at his watch. It was 6:02 PM. He went up to the microphone and turned it on. "We're leaving in a half hour to head to Jillian's to watch the game." He announced to everyone.

10

The Boston Fighting Cox were getting smoked in the 7th, 13-3 so some of the people decided to wonder off and play pool and video games. Bobby and Jack decided to stay at the bar and watch the game.

"We need to head down soon." Bobby commented. There were only ten fighters and Bobby. Five guys flaked for different reasons.

"Alright, I'll take five guys with me in five minutes and you come down with the rest in ten. Sound good?" Jack replied starting to stand and Bobby grabbed his arm.

"I'm not kidding, if I see someone in trouble, I'm jumping in." He said and let go of Jack's arm.

"I know, but I wish you wouldn't." Jack said walking away to grab five of the guys.

Ronnie stayed behind to have a couple more drinks with Bobby. "I think we'll be ok." He said.

"You don't even know how many people came, John wouldn't tell Jack." Bobby said guzzling his beer and putting his hand up for another.

"I know, but still I think you should have stayed back with the girls." Ronnie said wishing immediately he hadn't.

Bobby just stared at him and chugged his next beer. He put his hand up for another one and said, "I might be injured, old friend, but I'll still kick the shit out of you, no problem, so watch what you say."

Ronnie shut his mouth and wished he could have stayed back with the girls instead. His nerves were out of control. Fear and adrenaline were making him antsy. He wanted to fight right now instead of waiting, but knew he couldn't so he just ordered a shot.

Bobby was scared too, although he showed it a little better than Ronnie, he might even have been a little more scared. He knew he was falling for Stacey and that was exactly what he didn't want to happen, and he still had that bad feeling from earlier in the day.

He could feel the fear coming off of Ronnie which made him more edgy, since Ronnie was one of the better fighters. He had no idea how many people were fighting for the BSB and how well they all fought.

Bobby stepped out of Jillian's and was met with a September night chill. As he walked out from under the awning it started raining heavily. Just like in his dream it hurt his face and he could see his breath. He shook his head and said "Let's go," to the four guys who were with him.

He lit up a cigarette feeling his heart pounding as they reached the bridge. Bobby looked both ways and saw no signs of any movement. The game wasn't even over yet, but he knew most of the people would be leaving to try to beat traffic. It didn't matter either way, however, because the only thing people would come this way for was Jillian's and that was almost a mile away. He parted the fence and stepped through.

He led his group to the left where the rest of The Nation was waiting. Bobby could see various lit cigarettes through the darkness not too far in.

Jack came up and said, "A train just went by so we should have at least a half hour, right?"

"Should be, but I didn't check the schedule." Bobby replied feeling his heart slam off of his chest as the moment of truth got closer. "What time did you tell them to come?" He asked looking at his watch.

"I told them to come down at 11." He said.

"Alright, well it's 10:53." Bobby said out loud. "They'll be here any minute." He paused then looked at Jack, "They'll come earlier to try and beat us here. At least that's what I'd do."

The rain started coming down harder and Bobby felt his boots sink into the mud a little. Any buzz he could have gotten from all the drinks was gone. They were hidden by Jillian's and a group of trees, so that kind of put Bobby at ease, but the butterflies were still dog fighting each other in his stomach. He wanted to vomit, but not in front of everyone, so he just started taking deep breathes through his nose.

"When it starts I want you to fall back at least ten yards." Jack said breaking through Bobby's thoughts.

"Stop your worrying. I won't do anything unless I see the need to." Bobby said and actually meant it, which shocked Jack.

Just then they heard a "BSB" chant. It sounded like they had at least a million people. They all stared as one by one they came through the fence. Bobby counted seventeen people in all.

The BSB lined up in a straight line about five yards from where the FCN was lined up. As people's breathing quickened, the night seemed to fill up with fog all around Bobby, just like in his dream, and his stomach sank causing him to vomit in his mouth. He swallowed it back enough so it was just a mouthful and spit it out before he stepped back a few yards like he promised. His mind was in a fury and all of a sudden he was seeing things on a whole new level, he was more focused than he had ever been in his life.

"Nation!" Jack screamed and then started running causing everyone to follow suit.

Bobby singled out John because he screamed "BSB" and started running. Jack tackled John and got maybe two punches off before he was ripped off by another BSB member.

Jack squared up with him and threw a few haymakers that missed the target. The guy countered with a haymaker of his own that landed square on Jack's jaw knocking Jack to the ground.

John was on his feet now looking for another person to fight. Nick punched him in the back of the head knocking him back down and then kicked him hard in the back. Another BSB member grabbed John and pulled him off to the side before Nick could do anymore damage. After John was safely leaning on the fence, the guy jumped back in at

Nick. He grabbed the back of Nick's shirt and Nick elbowed him in the face, spraying blood out of his nose.

Jack was back on his feet, searching for someone. He kicked a guy who was tag teaming Jason in the back of the knee, then punched the other one in the throat sending him to his knees gasping for air. He grabbed the first guy by the back of his head and kneed him in the face. The guy went down like a ton of bricks.

A kid named Sam for The Nation was face down being kicked. Jack tackled one guy landing on top of him and laying a barrage of fists into the guys face. Another guy went to swing at Jack, but Jason caught the crook of the guys elbow with his. He put his left leg behind the guy's and violently threw him to the ground over his hip.

When the coast was clear Bobby ran in, grabbed Sam and brought him back. It hurt him to do so, but it was his only job and he was going to do it with perfection God damn it.

Sam was unconscious, but breathing. Bobby snapped his fingers and slapped him in the face a couple of times, bringing him back to.

"What happened?" He asked confused.

Bobby laughed and said, "You got knocked out my friend."

Jack was off the guy who was kicking Sam and was looking for someone else. His eyes were filled with rage. It seemed like everything was under control, the Bullies were starting to retreat, but his thirst wasn't quenched. He ran and jumped into the air kneeing the guy Ronnie was fighting in the head. Ronnie threw his arms up and yelled something, but Bobby couldn't hear it over the rain.

Bobby saw a few more guys who needed help getting off the battlefield so he hopped to it, grabbing people. His sides were killing him. He could only imagine what would happen if he had fought and silently thanked God that everyone gave him shit about it. He looked at his cousin, whose face was covered in blood and mud, and smiled.

The BSB were trying to retreat, but Jack wasn't having it. He had gone mad with rage and Bobby had to grab him and pull him away.

"What the fuck!" He screamed into Bobby's ear and elbowed him in the ribs, sending him to his knees in agonizing pain. "Oh shit, sorry Bobby." He said after he realized what he had done.

Nick helped Bobby to his feet laughing. "Didn't even fight and you get hurt? Damn Jack, aren't you the one who was afraid of this."

"Sorry Bobby, I guess I lost my mind a little." Jack said with a frown.

"Only a little, what the fuck man?" Bobby replied. "Let's go back to Razzy's. If anyone asks we played football." He said starting off towards the hole in the fence holding his side.

Once the FCN walked into Razzy's, everyone stopped talking and drinking and just stared at the group of muddy and bloody guys. They slowly parted as Jack led them to the back. Bobby was the last to walk in. Ruth looked at him hopeful from behind the bar. He nodded and smiled which in turn made her smile.

He walked to the bar to get a shot of whiskey, "Anything on the news?"

She shook her head. "No news is good news, right?"

"No news is what we want." He swung the shot back and put the glass down. "They know?" He asked nodding toward the crowd of people who were slowly starting their conversations back up.

"Some of them, I guess, but there are some in here who don't even know who the Fighting Cox are." She replied shrugging.

"That's good I suppose." He said and walked away.

In the back people were cheering and drinking. It was a select few people Nancy had allowed to the back. Anna found Jack and was touching his face. She smacked Ronnie in the arm since he was the closest person to her.

"I told you not to let anything happen to him!" She cried out.

"He lost his fucking mind. That right there," Ronnie said pointing to Jack's face, "That's all him."

Bobby shook his head and smiled. He didn't know why he had that dream, but he was glad nothing came of it. He felt a hand slither into his and he turned. It was Stacey looking anxiously at Bobby for signs of him fighting.

"Don't worry, I didn't fight." He said softly and led her to the bar still holding her hand as well as his ribs.

"Oh really?" She asked stopping suddenly causing Bobby to jerk, which caused more pain.

"Yes, really, what the fuck was that?" He retorted.

"Why are you holding you're fucking ribs if you didn't fight?"

"Stop being crazy," He said scolding her.

"That was Jack." Ronnie said laughing, trying to break the tension, "Bobby grabbed him because he wouldn't stop fighting and Jack elbowed him."

Stacey's cheeks turned red with embarrassment. "I'm sorry, Bobby, I was just worried about you."

He ignored her and sat at the bar. "Hey Nancy, could I get two shots of Jack, please?" He asked then looked at Stacey, who was sitting on the stool next to him like a kid who was caught with their hand in the cookie jar. "Make it four." He added.

They both took their shots in silence. She didn't want to upset him anymore than she already had and he just didn't want to talk to her, because he was afraid of what he'd say. There was a lot going through his head, but at the same time he couldn't tell you what it was.

He finally looked over at her and said, "I should actually be thanking you."

"Why is that?" She asked holding up four more fingers to Nancy.

"I was pulling people off to safety, sort of like a medic during a battle, and that alone made my sides hurt. I could only imagine what would have happened if I fought."

She smiled wide, "So maybe you'll start listening to me then?"

"Don't push your luck," He said taking one of the shots Nancy put out for them.

She shrugged, "I'll take what I can get,"

"I want to make a toast." Jack's voice came booming over the speakers. "Everyone who went out there tonight, I am proud of you. You guys kept your heads on a swivel and watched out for each other," He looked at Bobby, "Even you, cousin. I know how much you wanted to be out there fighting with us, but thank you for not fighting.

"I know you're all hurting, but let us all raise a glass. To Nancy, The Nation, the women loyal to The Nation and to the BSB, cheers."

Everyone said, "Cheers," throwing whatever they were drinking down their throats.

They all felt like they were on top of the world, which, they pretty much were. Well Jack was anyway. His little project to produce baseball firms was catching on like wild fire and his firm won their first bout. He would have to find out about the others, but the only one that mattered was his and they were unstoppable in his eyes.

11

Jack woke up not remembering anything after the speech he gave. He knew he was at his house, but how he got there was anyone's guess. Anna was in bed with him naked again and he had a raging headache.

He jumped in the shower and his face instantly burned. He shut the water off and looked in the mirror. He had a few cuts on his face, but they wouldn't scar. His bottom lip was split down the middle. He had a black eye and a bruise on his cheek. He touched the bruise and flinched at the pain.

He jumped back into the shower and endured the pain this time. The mud was still on his arms and somehow on his legs too, even though he wore pants. He had some scrapes on his legs, but other than that he was fine.

He threw on the towel and walked out to Bobby and Stacey sitting at his kitchen table.

"Jesus Christ!" He exclaimed, "You scared the fuck out of me."

"Door was unlocked so I let us in." Bobby said smiling. "I brought you guys' donuts and coffee from dunks."

"Thanks, man. Let me go put pants on." He went into his room only to emerge seconds later.

"How are you feeling?" Stacey asked. "You were throwing them back like it was water." She started chuckling.

"Like a truck hit me in the face." He replied taking a sip of coffee and pulling the cup back just as fast. He forgot about his lip. "Wish I had a painkiller or something"

Bobby went into his pocket. "Got you covered boss." He said handing him a bottle of Vicodin he'd had lying around his apartment from a back injury.

"Thanks man, you talk to anyone else yet?" He asked popping two pills.

"Yea, um, Jason told me to go fuck myself, Ronnie's on his way and Nick told me he hopes my cunt mother gets raped in the ass by a baseball bat." He said chuckling.

"At least I'm not the only one who feels like this." He said taking a bite of a chocolate frosted donut being careful of his lip this time.

"God you guys were fucking crazy last night." Stacey said laughing. "Or should I say early this morning. I thought Nancy was going to have to call the cops to get you out."

"What time did we leave?" Jack whispered.

"6:07." Bobby said looking at his phone, "I know because Nancy called me complaining that she was out a keg of beer, six liters of Jack and three liters of Smirnoff, and those were the ones you guys didn't drink."

"Jesus, what time is it now?" He asked.

"3:47"

"Fuck me." Jack groaned.

"That's not the worst part." Bobby said grinning from ear to ear.

"What is?" Jack moaned.

"We got another fight tonight."

"What the fuck do you mean? I thought that shit was over."

"Nah, man, you didn't answer your phone. We have a three game series and John is staying all three games. We got fights today and tomorrow. I warned all of you retards not to drink so much, but the good news is doc here cleared me as long as I get wrapped first." Bobby said putting an arm around Stacey.

"Dude, you're going too fast right now. Slow down." Jack said putting a hand up in defense.

Bobby laughed. "Stacey said that she didn't think I could hurt myself anymore than I already have, so if I let her wrap my ribs up with a couple rolls of Ace Bandage, then I can fight."

"That isn't true, I don't want him to fight, but he won't listen to me. I just figure if I wrap him up he'll get hurt less." She said shaking her head.

"Hold on." Jack said running to the bathroom. He was vomiting and it was loud.

"That's nasty." Anna said emerging from Jack's room.

"Hey sis," Stacey said.

"How could you let him get that drunk?" Bobby asked.

"Hey, I tried to stop him when Nancy threatened to call the cops. He's as stubborn as you sometimes."

"No I'm not, you just weren't persistent enough!" Jack exclaimed wiping his mouth with the back of his hand.

"Well since you were passed out, I had to meet with John over lunch."

"Why?" Jack asked.

"He wanted one and you weren't awake. Anyway, he just wanted to make sure there were no hard feelings about the other night and to make sure we're still on for tonight."

"You should have woke me up."

"I tried you asshole. You weren't waking up even when I was banging on your door for half an hour. Your dad came out thinking I was a robber."

"So how was my door unlocked just now?"

Bobby smiled and threw an unraveled paper clip on the table, "Learned that in the bricks," He replied talking about the Mystic Projects.

"Wait, isn't it an afternoon game today?" Jack asked, his words coming out slowly because he was trying not to throw up again, this time on his table.

"Yea, but we don't want to fight in the day time."

Ronnie walked in with Jason and Nick holding his head as he said, "I should have listened to you, Bobby; I don't want to move right now."

Bobby laughed. "I told you guys, but you didn't listen, who would have thought I'd be the mature one?"

They had their meeting as Stacey and Anna went into Jack's room to watch TV. They went around the table and said what they felt about last night. They all felt good as to how everything was handled. Sure, there were a few kinks, but they would work those out in time.

"Ok, now that that's out of the way, have a look at this." Bobby said throwing a national newspaper on the table. The headline was, *has hooliganism finally made its mark in the US?* There was a picture of a group of men being put into a paddy wagon.

"Apparently not everyone was as quiet about this as us. The Chicago firm fought the Tampa firm in front of Chicago's field and the Cleveland firm fought the Texas firm in front of a bar on a crowded street." Bobby said.

"Jesus Christ." Nick said. "Maybe you should get on that Facebook thing and tell everyone the rules or something Jack."

"I did," He replied, "but arrests were bound to happen eventually."

"Well they didn't get the memo." Bobby said. "I think you should set up like a higher order type thing with all the majors of every firm and have a meeting or something."

"That's not a bad idea. You showed John this?" Jack asked.

"Yea he was the one who came up with the order thing." Bobby said rising from his seat, "I set the meet up for eleven. I am going to go home I'll meet you guys at Jillian's at 9?"

"No Razzy's?" Jason asked.

"Well, I'll be going to Razzy's, but I don't think Nancy wants to see you guys." Bobby said laughing.

"Yea 9 sounds good I'm going back to bed. I'll call Nancy later and apologize." Jack said.

Everyone got up to leave then having the same idea as Jack. Everyone was hung over and just needed more rest, especially if they were going to fight tonight.

"They destroyed the fucking place." Nancy was telling Bobby when he walked into Razzy's with Stacey. "You know Saturday is my busy night now that the people know about karaoke and now I can't even open the back."

It was five PM and Razzy's was going to be on the verge of becoming packed, but right now, short for a few regulars, there was no one in there. Bobby didn't understand how they made any money at this hour, but that was none of his business. What was his business was the mess.

"Jesus, Mary and Joseph," He muttered as he stepped into the backroom.

The speakers were all flipped, along with every table not bolted to the wall. There was broken liquor bottles smashed against the wall with remnants of said liquor trying to make its way to the floor only to dry into a sticky mess. There was a keg imprinted into the wall on the stage with a bunch of chairs overturned in front of it along with holes in the walls throughout the room from heads, fists and feet.

Nancy walked over to where the keg was and said, "This was that big guy, I believe his name was Mike or Mark. It was his idea and he called it keg bowling. These holes," She was pointing to the walls, "Jason and Nick's idea of a 'man' contest. They were arguing about sleeping together or something."

"I'm gonna kill them." Bobby whispered.

"The broken liquor bottles," She pointed to the sticky residue on the wall, "That young kid Sam was walking back and forth and they all had target practice; one missed and destroyed my karaoke machine. I love your cousin, Bobby, but I think I am going to kill him."

"How much did you lose?" Bobby asked.

"It doesn't matter I can't charge him." She said shaking her head sounding a little defeated.

"Nancy, how much are the damages?" He asked persistently.

"Bobby, what does," She started, but Bobby stopped her.

"How much Nancy?" She could hear the anger rising in his voice.

"Not being able to open tonight, plus all of the damages and loss of alcohol? I would say a little over six thousand, but that's just a quick estimate." She replied.

"I'll pay you it back, Nancy, I promise." He said embarrassed for his cousin's actions. "Who would have thought I would have been the grown up. I'm sorry, really." He said sincerely.

"Aw, sweetheart, I appreciate that. Sometimes people get out of control." She said as Stacey handed her a check. "What's this hon?"

"A check for ten thousand, that should cover damages and at least some of the liquor you have been fronting us." She said with a smile on her face.

"What the fuck?" Bobby replied wide eyed.

"You said we would learn about each other eventually. Me and my sister are trust fund babies. I got way too much money." She said innocently.

"I thought your dad was a lawyer?"

"Yea, he's a partner at a huge firm and my mother is a brain surgeon, plus they invested their money really well."

"No, I can't take this from you. I just wouldn't feel right." Nancy said almost as shocked as Bobby.

"Please, Nancy, I would be offended if you didn't." Stacey said giving her the most innocent sweet face she could muster up.

"How can I say no to a face like that?"

"You can't." Bobby said still staring at Stacey wide eyed.

"You really have grown Bobby, so you better be smart enough to keep her." She hugged Stacey and walked out.

"We're gonna talk later you and I." Bobby said as he started to pick up chairs.

"There's nothing to talk about. Do you feel any different about me now that you know I'm rich?"

Bobby thought about it for a second. He grew up not having any money and worked for everything he had. He could easily have her pay for everything, but he was too proud and so he said, "No, no different. I just figured this would be something we would have discussed."

She gave him a provocative smile and just started helping with the cleanup. "Oh yea, don't tell Jack yet. I don't think Anna wants him to know."

"Ok, but if he asks I can't lie to him and you better tell Nancy not to say anything."

They finished cleaning up around six thirty and besides the holes and the ruined karaoke set, the place looked as good as it did before. Satisfied with their work, they went to the front to drink. It was starting to get crowded with people anxious to sing some karaoke.

Nancy had to get on the loud speaker, "Sorry ladies and gentlemen, tonight there will be no karaoke due to a malfunction in the machine."

People got upset with that, but there wasn't anyone too out of control. Bobby and Stacey sat at the end of the bar and drank, while shooting the shit with Ruth.

After an hour and a half people started getting restless and by now the bar was at max capacity. They were chanting that they wanted karaoke and yelling at Nancy. People started shoving each other while others sang the songs coming out of the juke box.

"I have never seen so many pissed off Yuppies." Bobby said to Ruth.

"Me either, but this might get bad quick." She said getting on the loud speaker. "The next round is on the house." She screeched.

"That won't help." Bobby said and it didn't. People stopped saying they wanted karaoke and started chanting, "Razzy's Sucks!"

One guy stood on top of the bar and started kicking glasses off of it. Bobby had had enough. He started to rise out of his chair and Stacey tried to grab him, but he pushed her hand away. He pushed a few people out of the way and grabbed the kid by his ankles sending him backwards smashing his head off of the bar. He pulled him off as hard as he could which sent him sprawling on the floor with a grunt.

A riot almost started, but Bobby held out his hand for the mic to the loudspeaker and said, "I swear to God I will fight every single one of you if you don't calm the fuck down. You might jump me, but I'll snap one or two of ya necks before I go down. Who wants to try their luck?" He pointed to one guy and asked, "You want it, buddy?" He snarled and the guy shook his head furiously. "This is a neighborhood bar and I'll be damned if I let a bunch of rich yuppies like you ruin it. As we speak Stacey over there," He pointed to her and she looked up confused, "Is texting a bunch of my friends, local kids, to come down and defend the bar you took away. So if you want a war then keep on going the way you are now." He looked around, waiting for someone to take a swing at him. When he was confident they were all calm he said, "Anything else you have trouble understanding, I'll be at the end of the bar drinking with my girlfriend." He handed the mic back to Ruth. The place was totally silent as he sat back down. After awhile most of the people got up and left.

"Thank you Bobby." Nancy said.

"I probably just scared off most of your business."

"That's ok. There is no way I'd want a bunch of spoiled punks in here who would start a riot because they couldn't sing karaoke."

He looked at Stacey who was smiling ear to ear. "What are you grinning at?" He asked.

"You said I was your girlfriend."

He just grunted and went back to drinking. He didn't mean to say it and didn't even realize he had said it until she mentioned it. He looked at his watch and it was almost eight.

When Bobby left Razzy's, there were only about ten people there. The rest of the people all staggered out at various times after Bobby's little debacle.

When he got to Jillian's, the place was packed. He got a text from John right as Jack showed up with Anna. It said *we want to hang out after the fight. You know just to show no hard feelings.*

"God, it's like he wants to fuck me or something." Bobby said.

"You ready?" Jack asked.

"You're late, I been ready." Bobby replied coldly.

"Yea, I'm still hung over. You wrapped up?"

"Yea, don't worry about me."

It was ten thirty and they were supposed to meet at eleven. "Drink up." Ronnie said placing shots in front of Jack and Anna. Jack gagged, but took the shot like a man.

"I feel your pain." Jason said pulling a seat up next to Jack.

"Nancy was pissed, but it's all taken care of." Bobby said.

"Oh?" Jack replied questioningly.

"Yea, what the fuck were you guys thinking?"

"I wish I knew what you're talking about, but I don't remember anything."

"The damage was like six."

"Hundred?"

"Thousand, also, you fucked up her karaoke machine and it almost started a riot."

"How did that turn out?"

"Bobby fucked some guy up." Stacey chimed in absentmindedly as she sipped on her sex on the beach. They all looked at her and she shrugged. "What? He did."

"We need to set something up. Like a meeting or something, between all the majors. Now I figure we can break it up into different sections, but you're the boss." Bobby said.

"Yea we can talk to John later. Maybe we can go have a meet with him or something." Jack replied diplomatically.

"We're all gonna meet up at Razzy's. We can talk to him then." Bobby replied. "Don't worry about Nancy, like I said I," He paused and looked at Stacey, "We took care of it." She smiled and played with her hair.

"Thank you." Jack replied more to Stacey than Bobby.

The one thing Jack had over Bobby was his level of maturity. Jack was always the mature one and now it was as if the rolls were reversed. His jealousy, he hated to say, was becoming a little too unbearable.

"You're welcome." She said and smiled. She was about to say what Bobby said about her being his girlfriend, but she didn't want to push him back away now that they were as close as they were.

They all got up to leave and Bobby kissed Stacey on the head and whispered, "Your secret is safe with me, but you might want to tell Anna you told me."

Jack kissed Anna deeply and followed Bobby to the exit and the rest of The Nation followed suit. It was an odd spectacle, seeing all these people walk out in a single file line. This time Bobby knew the only cops they would encounter were the ones guarding Jillian's, so there were no worries about being caught.

When they couldn't see them anymore Stacey turned to Anna. "Bobby knows that we're rich."

"You told him?" She almost yelled.

"It was out of my control, but don't worry he wont tell Jack."

"Are you sure?"

"I trust him," She paused and looked around to make sure Kerry and Lisa weren't near and whispered, "He called me his girlfriend." They giggled like school girls and Stacey quickly said, "Don't say anything yet."

They all entered the train tracks at 10:55. This time there were no butterflies in anyone's stomach. Bobby was wrapped up, but it felt weird. His mobility wouldn't be a hundred percent. More like in the fifties, low sixties at best.

The Nation stood waiting, wanting to get it over with more than anything, because they were all still hung-over. There was still mud from the night before, but it was starting to harden from the chill. The night was silent and creepy.

This time the BSB walked through the fence quietly. Whether they didn't want to bring attention to themselves or their morale was down, Bobby would never know.

This time they didn't wait, the BSB ran at The Nation right when they were clear of the fence. A lot of The

Nation wasn't paying attention and were caught by surprise. John superman punched Jack in the face sending him to the ground unconscious.

One of the guys tried a jumping spin kick at Bobby, but missed him entirely and fell to the ground. Bobby ceased the opportunity, jumping on top of the guy throwing punches until the guy was limp. He got up and most of The Nation was already down.

He squared up with John, but another guy grabbed him from behind letting John lay a barrage of hay makers into his face. Even though the punches weren't hard, Bobby thought he would soon submit to unconsciousness, until John said, "That's enough." And the other guy let him drop to his knees. "You said Razzy's in Somerville, right?" He asked Bobby.

"Yea, you can head there now if you want, but it's obviously going to take us a little while." He replied looking up at John and wiping the blood from his nose. "I'll call them and let them know you guys are coming now, so they can put a bartender in the back room."

John held out his hand to help Bobby to his feet. He accepted it willingly enough. They shook hands and John, along with the rest of the BSB, walked back through the fence. Only one of them needed help, the one Bobby knocked out. The rest were fine.

Bobby walked over to Jack and started smacking him in the face. Jack finally came to and asked, "We lose?"

"Yea, we got the shit kicked out of us and it only took a couple of minutes." Bobby replied helping him to his feet.

"Now help me get the rest of them up so we can go drink with them at Razzy's." He walked off to call Nancy.

Jack walked over to Jason, who wasn't unconscious, only out of breath, and helped him to his feet. Jason in turn went to Nick, while Jack went to Ronnie and it only took a few minutes for everyone to be up and ready to leave.

"Nancy's pissed." Bobby said walking back.

"Why?" Jack asked holding his head.

"It's because of you fucking assholes. She doesn't want to let us back there, but I convinced her to let us."

They walked back to Jillian's to meet up with the girls. Anna and Stacey were both visibly upset. "Jesus Christ, Jack." Anna said grabbing for his face. He pulled back, but she wouldn't let go.

"Don't get too drunk tonight you morons." Bobby said as they formed a circle around the girls. He looked at each and every member in turn and then spit up blood that was festering in his mouth. "That's supposed to be our bar. Our fucking home and you guys decided to destroy it." He turned and walked off lighting a cigarette, with Stacey hot on his trails.

"Jesus Christ, what's his fucking problem?" Ronnie asked.

"I don't know, but he's right." Jack said putting his arm around Anna's waist. "We were a fucking disgrace tonight. We have a rep to protect and tonight," He paused and looked out at his bloody and beaten Nation, "Tonight we let them spit on it."

"Fuck!" Jason screamed into the night with pain and anguish in his voice. Where they were from, what made you a man was your reputation of being tough and your word. If you had a reputation for getting your ass kicked, well then, you weren't a man.

Everyone put there heads down in shame. "It's alright guys; just don't ever let it fucking happen again." Jack said. He grinned and his teeth were stained red with blood. "Now let's go get fucked up with the people who just beat our asses." He started off, but paused, "But not too fucked up, unless you want to be fighting Bobby tonight. He's a little upset about us messing up Razzy's."

While Jack and the rest of The Nation were getting on the train, Bobby and Stacey were getting out of a cab in front of Razzy's. It was expensive, but Bobby didn't want to be on public transportation with a bunch of drunken idiots right now or the FCN and despite his protests, Stacey ended up paying for cab.

He stepped into Razzy's, packed like any normal Saturday despite the earlier events, and Nancy pointed them to the back, it was closed off for them. Nancy followed him and stopped him in between the two rooms.

"Bobby, I don't know how long this can go on for. Most of my money comes in from this back room. Once the room is fixed up again you guys can have Monday through Thursday, but Friday, Saturday and even Sunday," She paused.

"I know, Nancy, we appreciate it and if we want to come back here, we'll do it as paying customers, with your paying customers. No more private bullshit." He said and walked into the room.

The room had an awkward feeling that Bobby didn't like too much. He scanned the room and people were spread out filling all the tables up. Whether it was planned by John, or on accident, Bobby didn't know. Even a few of the BSB sat alone at tables.

Everyone just stopped talking and stared at him. He didn't see John anywhere. He turned the corner and he was alone at the bar talking to Nancy's son Joey, who would be manning the bar for this shindig. Bobby walked over to him and held out his hand. Once John shook it vigorously he finally sat down.

He looked at Joey and said, "I think your mom was looking for you. We should be fine back here for now." He watched Joey until he disappeared around the corner. "We need to talk business, but not until Jack gets here."

"That's understandable. He is, after all, your major, hey Chris!" He called out over the loud conversation that started back up. A big burly guy got up and walked over. It was the guy who had held Bobby as John took free swings. "Bobby, let me introduce you to my right hand man Chris. We grew up together."

Chris held out his hand to Bobby and he shook it respectively. "No hard feelings?" He asked

"Nah, it's all in good fun." Bobby replied. "For now, anyways," He added with a teasing smile.

"We didn't mean to be rude by taking up all of the tables. We just figured we could all get to know each other better if they were forced to sit with each other." John said.

"I would like it if everyone doing this could get along. This, for me anyways, is more like a hobby. Something fun to do, you know what I mean?" Bobby replied.

"That's how we feel as well." Chris said, "You fight and then buy each other a drink, like the old days."

"I'll drink to that," Bobby said reaching over the bar and grabbing the bottle of Jamison along with three shot glasses. He poured the whiskey and handed it out and they all drank.

"I don't mean to pry, but what the hell happened to this place." John asked.

"The boys kind of got out of control last night." Bobby replied. When the both of them just looked at him confused he told the story of how The Nation destroyed the bar.

By the time he was done Joey had come back with a pitcher of beer for the three of them and Jack and the rest of The Nation finally showed up.

Jack sat down next to Bobby and everyone else kind of stood awkwardly. "We should tell everyone to leave so we can talk privately." Bobby said. "Not that it's a private conversation, but we could hear each other better."

"Bullies," John yelled, "Go to the other bar real quick!"

"You too, Nation," Jack yelled. Stacey and Anna stayed behind with Lisa and Kerry standing by loyally. "Sorry ladies, that means you too."

Once everyone was gone they all got up and walked to a table with their pitcher and four frozen cups.

"Now, the first order of business is how to go about organizing this." John said taking a swig of beer then putting his glass back down, "any ideas," He finished.

"I thought about it, but came up with nothing. You think of anything Bobby?" Jack asked.

"Well," Bobby started, leaning in close. "In baseball, there are two leagues, East and West, which are both divided by three divisions, East, Central and West. I figure we can do basically the same thing. How many teams have firms now?" He asked turning to Jack.

"Every team has a firm now." Jack replied curiously.

"Right, so we just keep the divisions that the MLB has and each division governs themselves." Chris, John and Jack all looked lost so Bobby got flustered. "Ok, for example, we would be American League East. Jack, John and the majors for Toronto, New York and Tampa would govern American League East, same thing for American League Central and West. Then each division would vote for one major to represent that Division and same for each League. I mean it isn't perfect, but it should work for now and we could always improvise in the future."

"That actually makes sense." Chris said.

"Thank you, I thought about it all night."

"Ok good, now as for weapons." John said.

"No guns or anything of that sort." Chris said

"Agreed," Jack replied.

"How do we have meetings between each other?" John asked, still hung on Bobby's idea.

"Well, we would have to set up a location in between each place. I mean if it's ok with everyone else, we could meet up with Tampa in like Virginia or something." Jack said.

"Good, only majors and right hand men allowed." John replied.

"This is going well." Bobby stated, and then said, "Joey another pitcher, please."

"So, Jack, how did this come about, you know making firms?" Chris asked.

"Well, Bobby here had gotten into it with a Minutemen fan and shit turned sour when he put him in the hospital," He started.

"We know how all that went down," John said, "Why do you think I didn't hit you in the ribs Bobby? How did you actually come up with this idea?"

"I appreciate that, John. You're a stand up guy." Bobby replied genuinely gratefully.

"Oh, well, we ended up watching *Green Street Hooligans* and thought how awesome it would be if we did it, so we did." Jack said as Joey put the pitcher in front of them. "Is that all the business we need to discuss?"

"Yea I think that pretty much covers it." John replied.

"Good, do you think you could go get our men and ladies Bobby?" Jack asked.

"Yea boss."

"You too Chris," John said. Each major was trying to prove the better man.

"Yea, no problem," He replied and they both left.

"You guys showed good faith and trust coming here, I appreciate it really I do." Jack was saying as each firm made their way back in wary of each other.

"Let's make a toast." Jack said as loud as he could, raising his beer up high. "To our new friends from Baltimore, it's been a pleasure."

Everyone raised their glasses hesitantly and all yelled, "Cheers!" in unison.

Ronnie had pulled Bobby aside as if something was eating at him. "What's the matter?" Bobby asked.

"It's Jack. What is all this friendly shit? I mean, come on Bobby, we should be enemies. Friends don't fight each other." Ronnie replied

"Don't worry. We're not friends, Jack is just being friendly, there's a difference." Bobby said reproachfully. "Jack is our major and maybe sometimes his ideas are flawed, but this time I think his head is in the right place and besides, friends do fight each other."

"Well you may be the only one who agrees with him. I'm not talking about just us either. They were saying the same shit down there," He replied nodding to the BSB, "and only close friends fight each other."

Bobby looked at him with pure malevolence and said, "I hope to God you're not implying a mutiny, my friend, because I will kill all of you."

"No!" Ronnie almost screeched. "It's just that, I don't want it to come to that. I'm just trying to tell you what everyone else is feeling."

"Go have a shot on me." He simply replied and went to find Jack.

Ronnie immediately got a bad feeling in the pit of his stomach, but Bobby wouldn't tell Jack what Ronnie had just said, no, he had enough to worry about.

12

"I have to ask you a question." Stacey said to Bobby.

"What is it?" He replied.

Bobby wanted to show her his favorite place in the world, so after they left Razzy's early, he drove over to the Prospect Hill Tower and brought her up the steps to see the breathtaking view of the Boston skyline. She gasped and he smiled. It was nice to share this with someone he was falling in love with, although he wouldn't admit that out loud, not yet at least. They were now sitting on the wall with their legs hanging over the drop.

"How do you keep your body that," She grasped for the right words, "Well, um, chiseled?"

He looked at her with a crooked grin, "I was shot with this experimental drug when I got out of high school. It would make my body look like this forever." He shrugged, "I needed the money."

"Bobby I'm serious. You drink, smoke and eat a lot. I never see you work out and yet, you have this amazing body. I'm sorry it just amazes me," She shrugged, "that's all."

"Well before I hurt myself I was doing one thousand push ups and sit ups a night and I would run the Mystic

River after work every day. I guess I'll go back to doing that when all this madness slows down a little."

"Can I run the river with you?" She asked shyly, "You know when you start again."

"I'm not sure you can keep up." He said shoving against her gently with his shoulder.

She looked into his eyes, "You have beautiful eyes Bobby. If you grew up somewhere else I don't think you would even know how to fight. No, there, you would be a ladies man, probably a model."

"Well were not there, I'm here and all I know how to do is fight."

"I'll break through that rock exterior you got going on. I will get you to open up to me."

"Maybe, but not tonight," He replied smiling.

"So are we a couple?" She asked not wanting to bring it up, but wanting to know.

"I don't know if you can handle me Stacey." He said not wanting to be rude.

"What the fuck is that supposed to mean?"

"I do what I want when I want. I take offense when someone tries to tell me what to do." He stopped as a breeze picked up and lifted her hair softly off of her shoulders, bringing a fresh scent of the Vitoria's Secret Sexy perfume she was wearing to his nose. He loved the smell of it, "I think I might like you, but I don't want you to end up hating your life because of me." He put his head down in shame.

"Stop that Bobby." She said and he gave her a confused look. "I don't know what your fucking problem is, but you stop trying to make me feel sorry for you and you stop being afraid to get close to someone!" Bobby said nothing for a few minutes then she lowered her voice. "You can't go through life by yourself and I'm not just talking about me either. You are also put off with Jack for some reason," She paused a moment then said, "That's not right, it's like you're trying to take on the world by yourself and trying to make sure that Jack's life isn't somehow fucked up by what you do, like he's never seen a fight before."

"Stacey, what are you talking about?" He asked.

"Remember that fight with Jackie G?" He nodded, "Well I asked you to bring people, your cousin wanted to go, but you were too stubborn to bring anyone and you fucked yourself up. What good did that do you? It didn't make you look more like a man. You looked like a fucking idiot."

"I'm trying Stacey. I really am, but,"

She cut him off. "I see that Bobby, but you're not trying hard enough." She swung her legs around off the wall and jumped down.

"Stacey." She turned back to him, "Will you go out with me?"

"Don't do me any favors Bobby." She said and walked home. He probably could have stopped her, but he chose to let her go instead and give her some space.

Jack stumbled into his door and hit his face. He fell down laughing. "Jesus Christ Jack, not again." Anna said trying to pick him up. He mumbled some incoherent drunk talk and Anna reached in his pants to find his keys.

She got him inside and into bed, but he was scaring her. Every night he wanted to drink. He stopped going to work and tried to get Anna to stop going to school.

He started mumbling something else that she couldn't understand. "What did you say?" She asked, but he just turned his head and started dry heaving. She ran into the kitchen to get a trash bag and made it just in time to catch his throw up mostly in the bag, but some on her shirt.

She started dry heaving and knew it was enough. After she ran into the bathroom to throw up she called Bobby. "Sorry if I woke you Bobby, but I need to talk to you about Jack."

"What's the matter?" He asked nervously.

"He's out of control. He won't stop drinking and he won't go to work. He's trying to make me stay home from school." She said sounding exhausted.

"Where is he now?" Bobby asked.

"He's throwing up in his bedroom. Where's Stacey?"

"I don't know she won't answer my phone calls. Maybe you'll have better luck?"

"Yea, I'll try and call you back."

She hung up and immediately dialed Stacey. "Where are you?" She asked when Stacey answered.

"Bobby's," She replied sounding like she just woke up.

"I just talked to him. He said he didn't know where you were."

"Yea I walked to his house from Prospect Hill. We got into an argument, if you can call it that, and I just walked here."

"Ok, well I'm going to ask him to come grab me, because I can't stay here." She said hanging up before Stacey could say anything else.

"Bobby can I stay at your place," She almost begged into the phone when Bobby answered. "I'm too tired to go home and you live closer."

"Wait, what would Stacey and Jack think?" He asked.

"Stacey's at your house and as far as I can see Jack won't be saying anything for awhile." She replied.

"Well, ok, you're at Jack's?" He asked not liking this idea one bit.

"Yes and he's passed out and I have puke all over my shirt."

"Ok, well I think Stacey has some extra clothes at my house and you can use my shower."

Bobby left Prospect Hill and picked her up, but right away things felt wrong. He felt like they were both cheating on Jack and he had no idea why. She was right, though; Jack was becoming a different person entirely. He was drinking too much, he was jealous of Bobby for some reason and he stopped going to work. He would need to talk to him and this would not end well. Jack would probably try to fight him, but Bobby saw no other way to approach this.

Anna got into his car and just smiled. "Thank you Bobby."

He grunted, afraid to say anything, thinking it would make him feel worse than he already did. As he turned onto Mystic Ave, which was dead this early in the morning, a voice spoke up in his head telling him to stop. He mentally told himself to shut the fuck up. He would not feel bad because Jack was being an asshole.

"Can I borrow your lighter?" Anna asked softly. For some reason they stopped selling cars that came with the lighter and Bobby just never got one. He dug into his pocket and pulled out both his lighter and cigarettes. She lit her cigarette taking in the harsh smoke and exhaled saying, "Thank you, again."

Bobby took the lighter back and lit his in turn. "I'm sorry if I seem rude, but Jack has got me fucked up and I have no idea why." He tried to explain, but thought he sounded dumb.

"I know what you mean. I don't mean to pry, but what happened with you and Stacey?" She asked

"It's complicated." He replied simply

"Please, Bobby, let's just break this tension." She pleaded.

"Ok, well bottom line is, she wants a relationship and I just can't put her through it." He said banging a U-turn on Mystic to head back to Medford.

"What do you mean?" She asked.

"Ah, now that's the complicated part." He replied putting his finger up.

"Cut the bullshit Bobby. What are you really afraid of?" She asked sternly.

"I'm not afraid of anything. I just know how I am and can't, in all good conscience, put your sister through that."

"Did you ever think that maybe she wants to be put through that? Maybe likes you so much and so intent on getting to know you that she'd go through hell and back just to do it?"

"No, I just," He stopped not knowing what else to say.

"Just give it a shot. Who knows Bobby? Maybe you two will end up in love." Bobby looked over to her smiling brightly.

"Can I be honest with you?" He asked emotionally.

"Yes of course."

"I'm afraid, because I think that I am in love with her already." He said shaking his head.

She gasped. "Big Bobby Cross afraid, I don't believe it!"

"It's true, but that stays between us, ok?"

She just nodded as he pulled into a parking spot on High Street. The night had a chill, but it wasn't too cold, to Bobby it felt weird again.

Stacey was sitting on his couch watching TV when they walked in. She didn't so much as raise her head in acknowledgement.

"Hey, sis, you got any extra clothes here?" Anna asked.

"In my bag, it's in the bedroom." She said with her eyes still focused on the show she was watching.

"Towels are in that closet." Bobby said pointing to his linen closet next to the bathroom. After he heard the shower turn on, he went and sat down next to Stacey. "I need to talk to you."

"I don't want to hear it anymore Bobby." She said coldly.

"Please." He begged in an innocent sounding voice.

"Fine," She said exasperated, turning off the TV.

"Listen," He started, but couldn't find the words. It felt like an eternity went by, Stacey waiting impatiently, before he continued, "I would love to be with you, officially, but I can't put you through it."

Before he could continue she snapped as tears fell down her cheeks, "Oh Bobby you're an idiot. Can't you see that I don't care who you used to be? I don't care how tough you are and I don't care how sorry you feel for yourself. The person under all of that is the sweetest man I have ever met. Your intentions are well, but you're an idiot. You're so afraid of Jack getting hurt that you faced eight men by yourself and got your ass kicked for all of your trouble."

"I know." He said wiping a tear from her cheek leaving his hand there for a moment letting her hair fall over it. She tried to look down, but he held his grip firm then leaned in and kissed her deeply. "I'm afraid of the way you make me feel." He whispered.

"How is that?" She whispered back.

"When I'm with you I feel safe, vulnerable even. I have never felt this way with anyone, not even my mother, from what I can remember. I feel like when I'm with you I could settle down and start a family and that's what scares me." He replied.

"Why would that make you scared?"

"My whole life I have been in control of everything. There has never been once when I haven't known what my outcome was or known somewhat of the outcome. I guess what I'm trying to say is if I go out with you and fall in love, like I know I will, then that leaves it open for me to get hurt." He put his head down in shame, and why not? He *was* being stupid, after all.

"You wouldn't want to take that chance with me?" She asked.

"Yes I would." He paused, finally determined to man up, "Stacey, will you be my girlfriend?" He asked raising his head.

She smiled, "Yes, I would love to Bobby."

They didn't hear the shower shut off or the bathroom door open, but Anna was standing there in a towel with her hands up to her face saying, "Awe you guys that was cute."

Bobby scrambled to the closet where she had originally gotten the towel and grabbed the quilt he kept up there, which was given to him by his grandmother, and threw it on the couch. "I'll sleep out here and you two can have my bed."

"No way, pal," Anna said and Bobby gave her a questioning look, "I'm not going to sleep on the bed where you and my sister knock boots." She chuckled. "I'll sleep on the couch, its fine."

Bobby didn't know what to do, so he just stood there awkwardly while Anna stood not two feet away in only a towel, until Stacey grabbed his arm and brought him into the bedroom smiling.

They made love all night, no not night, all morning and Bobby got no sleep.

13

Bobby made sure Stacey had fallen asleep before he got up. He got dressed quietly and walked into the living room where Anna was softly snoring up a storm. He lifted his car keys off of the key ring holder he had mounted to the wall and Anna's snoring faltered. He went a little slower gritting his teeth. Once her snoring was back on pace he opened the door and shut it quietly.

It was 7 AM and he was exhausted, but he had shit to do and so he went to the Dunkin Donuts on Mystic next to the Harrow's, a place that supposedly serves the best chicken pot pie which Bobby had never tried. He bought the Herald from the teenager selling them for two dollars, it was Sunday, and went in for a coffee and doughnut.

He placed the Herald upside down on a table before he ordered. Once he got his large hazelnut with cream and sugar and his Boston Kreme donut he sat back down. He lifted the lid to blow on the coffee then took a sip as he flipped the paper over and almost spit it everywhere, but held it in.

Right there on the front page was a huge picture of Nick punching one of the BSB's in the face. He read the caption, *Hooligans strike again on Somerville Ave in Somerville.* He was speechless, at what time did this happen? Who authorized it? How the fuck was it already in the paper!

He started reading; *Cops got called to a disturbance on Somerville Ave in the early hours at 12:15 AM. The unknown assailants fled the scene, but a couple of witnesses say they were two hooligan gangs. One was from Boston and the other from Baltimore, MD. Police have no suspects at this time. If anyone can identify the man in the picture from above then they are urged to call the Somerville police department a.s.a.p., continued on page 59.*

continued on page 59.

Bobby didn't flip the page to read the rest. Instead he called Nick. The phone rang four times and finally went to voicemail. He called Jason next, then, when there was no answer he tried Ronnie. No answer there either. Aggravated he threw his donut out and ordered another coffee, this one regular.

He threw the paper on the seat of his car before he jumped in and headed to Jack's.

When he got to Jack's the clouds parted and the sun came out a little. Even though it was cold, the sun felt good. He planned on going into Jack's room and just freaking out on him, but for some reason he decided to change his mind and rethink his approach.

He opened Jack's door and slammed it as hard as he could and a groan rose up out of Jack's room. He went into the room where Jack was half on the bed and half in the trash bag puking.

When he was finished Bobby said, "Get in the shower." Jack tried to protest, but Bobby said, "Now," persistently.

Jack looked up and said, "Leave me the fuck alone man. I don't want to fight today."

Bobby walked out of the room to the kitchen and Jack heard water running. Bobby walked back in and splashed cold water all over Jack. "Get in the shower now, Jack, or I'll keep doing this."

"Fuck you asshole." Jack said and then put his head back in the bag.

Bobby left again and came back splashing another bucket of cold water, this time with ice in it, onto Jack. He screeched like a wounded animal and pulled his covers back over himself.

"All day, Jack," Bobby said walking back into the kitchen.

"Ok! Ok!" Jack screamed getting up. He walked into the kitchen, shouldering Bobby, then into the bathroom.

Miraculously, Bobby only got water on Jack's bed. He took the trash bag full of vomit and threw it outside into the trash can. Jack got all of his puke in the bag and on Anna, also a miracle. Bobby stripped the bed and threw the blankets and sheets into a pile to throw into the wash and that was the gist of the damage.

Bobby sat at the table and lit a cigarette waiting for Jack. He was stubbing out his cigarette when Jack finally emerged saying, "What the fuck was so important that it couldn't wait until later?"

"Get dressed you're going to my house." He replied coldly.

"Why? Fuck you!"

"Just do it Jack."

"Tell me what's going on first."

"Fine, first you need to apologize to Anna."

"What are you talking about?"

"What is going on with you lately?" He asked ignoring Jack.

"Nothing, what the fuck are you trying to say?" He asked taking offense.

"You don't do anything anymore. When is the last time you went to work?"

"How is that your business?"

"What do you have against me? What happened all of a sudden?" When Jack stayed quiet Bobby knew it was his chance. "Jack, you're my best friend and I thought I was yours. What the hell is going on?"

"I, I don't know. I'm jealous of you, always have been." He looked around as if searching for an answer. "I think this Fighting Cox Nation thing is going downhill fast and I don't know if I can do anything about it."

"Jack, you need to sit down, read this and drink your coffee, then get dressed and meet me in the car." Bobby said getting up.

When Jack finally got in Bobby's car it was twenty minutes later. He looked worse than he did earlier, if that was possible.

"Were you there?" Bobby asked putting his car in gear.

"I honestly can't remember Bobby." Jack said confused. "I was so drunk and the last thing I remember is when John was singing." John had been singing, but not on the karaoke machine since it was broken, no he was singing acapella. A horrible rendition of "Who let the dogs out".

"Ok," Bobby said thinking out loud, "we need to talk to Anna first and see what she says. Then if you didn't ok it we need to apologize to John."

"I should have let you be major." Jack said embarrassed.

"It's ok I think I like it better this way anyway, since I get no blame." He looked over at Jack who was looking out the window absently and said, "Could be worse, man, you could be hooked on them OC's like a lot of the other people around here. You remember Chris Carr?"

"Yea, the captain of the hockey team our junior year?"

"Yea he overdosed a couple weeks back. He's dead. Booze is easier to kick then OC's"

"It's not that simple. I got depressed and started drinking. You don't think I know you'd be the better major? Or that you get more girls? Thinking of all that and the fact that you could get with Anna just fucked me up. I don't know what else to tell you."

"You want another coffee?" Bobby asked already pulling into Dunks, "You were always a better man than I was, brother, that's why I could never get with Anna and why I've been jealous of you."

Anna and Stacey were still asleep when they walked in and it was only eight thirty so there was really no rush to find out what happened.

Jack walked over and snuggled up with Anna on the couch, "I'm mad at you." She said to him somehow knowing it was his arms wrapping around her stomach.

"I'm mad at myself baby. Could you ever forgive me?" He asked kissing the back of her neck.

Bobby basically collapsed into bed. Stacey mumbled something about her doggie getting eaten by a mouse and threw her arm over him. He didn't feel it because he was already out cold.

When Bobby woke up Jack was sitting on the edge of the bed looking refreshed and startling Bobby.

"What the fuck man!" He shrieked. "What time is it?"

"Almost noon," He said looking at his watch, "I talked to Anna."

Bobby sat up interested. "What did she say?"

"We were out of the bar before that all happened."

"That's good. Now have you gotten a hold of Nick?"

"Yea, he said that the BSB started it. I also called John who said that Jason started with one of his guys."

"What did Jason say?"

"Now this is where it gets interesting. Apparently Lisa was flirting with the guy from BSB, his name is Rory, and then he saw Jason and Lisa kissing and totally flipped out. Apparently he started a fight in Razzy's. I confirmed this with Ruth."

"So they started it and are now denying it?" Bobby asked trying to rub the sleep out of his eyes.

"Apparently, but Bobby, he said they would come at us full force tonight." He paused shaking his head, not wanting to finish his sentence.

"What is it?" Bobby asked.

"Last night one of their men died. Mike punched him and he hit his head off of a curb and cracked his skull open."

"Shit," Bobby replied

"Yea, it was that guy Chris's brother."

"What the fuck does that mean?"

"I don't know, but it doesn't sit to well with me."

"Me either." He replied and pulled the covers off of himself, "Let's go meet with Jason, Nick and Ronnie."

"No, you go back to bed, I just wanted to let you know I'm trying, I also got my job back and Anna took your car to get breakfast with Stacey. I'll be in the living room." Jack said getting up and walking out.

Bobby just stared at him amazed. He had taken full responsibility and was trying to fix it, it was the Jack he knew and loved. He rolled back over and pulled the blankets up over his head and passed back out.

Stacey woke him two hours later. She was pulling his pants down.

"What time is it?" He asked groggily.

"Shh, don't worry, everything is taken care of and now it's your turn to be taken care of." She started taking her shirt off.

"Wait, where's Jack?"

"Took your car and is meeting with everyone. He said to tell you to rest up for tonight." She slid his erection into her and he had no more fight left in him.

Jack had called the meeting at his house. He ordered a couple of pizzas from Pini's while he waited for them to show up. Jason came in first sporting a black eye. "I know you didn't ok it, but we had to." He promptly tried to explain, but Jack just put his hand up.

"Wait for everyone to be here," Was all he said, taking a slice of pepperoni pizza.

While Bobby was asleep, he and Anna had come up with a plan that would take some of the load off of Jack. He was still the major, but Bobby would be the only one who dealt business with him. In turn Ronnie, Nick and Jason would be the only ones who did business with Bobby. Ronnie, Nick and Jason would deal with two members of the firm, each, until more people joined.

Nick showed up next. His face looked like it had just met a baseball bat and was barely recognizable. Before he could say anything Jack said, "Take a seat and let's wait for Ronnie."

"Where's Bobby?" Nick asked, sounding nervous for some reason.

"Ah, don't worry about him. Want a slice?" He asked tossing the box of pepperoni at him.

Nick and Jason both took a slice slowly. It was almost as if they were meeting with their mob boss and they had just fucked up a hit. Jason thought about how Jack's smile looked. It was all wrong, like he was fighting the urge to kill someone.

Ronnie finally strolled in looking pretty with no marks on his face at all. He took a seat without being asked. He had his badass face on and wouldn't budge an inch for any of them. "Let's get started." He said doing a poor job of masking the fear in his voice.

"Why do you guys look scared?" Jack asked in a firm, even voice.

"Listen, it was my fault, I know I fucked up." Nick replied.

"I didn't say anything about that so why bring it up?" Jack said turning his smile into a semi frown.

"Sorry man." Nick said.

"Relax. I called you guys here, because I came up with a governmental type thing." Jack said with the smile returning to his face. Nobody said anything for a moment so Jack went on, "You three, from now on, will talk with Bobby about anything businesslike and he'll bring it to me himself. I am going to give you each two of the fighters that will be under you. They report to you and only you for business." He pointed to Ronnie and said, "You have Stubbs and big Mike." Stubbs was his nickname because of his height. He was 5'4" with a Napoleon complex and big Mike was the one who decided to play keg bowling. It was kind of comical if you thought about it. Stubbs was 5'4" while Mike was 6'7" at the least.

"So do I have meetings with them or something?" Ronnie asked.

"If you want to, this is just for right now to take some of the pressure off of me. As we get bigger, you'll probably get more guys." He pointed to Nick. "You will get Rick and Matt." Rick was the older man of the group. He was only thirty two, but they all called him Pops to bust his balls. He was loyal as a dog too. Matt was their age, but wasn't from Somerville. He came down from New Hampshire when he heard the call. He might not be the toughest guy, but he never backed down from anything.

"Jason, you get Sam and Sean." Sam was the youngest of the group and still learning how to really fight and Sean was just fucked in the head. He was even crazier than Bobby. A better fighter than him though? Now that was a different story. "I will announce all of this later at Razzy's"

"Are we fighting tonight?" Ronnie asked.

"What do you think we should do?" Jack asked sitting back in his chair and crossing his arms.

"I think we should. Present a united front."

"Nah, I don't like that." Jason said. "We need to regroup and get our heads focused."

"I agree with Jason, but what do you say Nick?" Jack asked pleased with how this was going.

"I don't think we should fight either," he looked at Ronnie, "Sorry man, but I think Jason's right."

"Hey, it's whatever to me. I just don't like knowing that they think they got us scared or something." Ronnie said folding his hands behind his head.

Jack looked at his watch and said, "Ok, I will go talk to Bobby and see you guys at Razzy's around 8, how's that sound?"

"Good." Ronnie said.

"One more thing guys," Jack said as he rose out of the chair. He put his fists on the table, leaned in and said, "Don't ever fuck up like that again." They looked up with shocked expressions and Jack continued, "Yea we're boys, but that friendship ends when we start talking about business and I picked you three because I thought I could trust you. Do not make me regret it." He looked mostly at Ronnie and when no one said anything he continued, "Don't fuck up and we can be cool, now eat pizza and lock the door when you leave," He paused and said, "I don't know which one of you idiots started this, but someone's dead now because of it." He picked up a slice and started eating it, while he walked out.

"What a dick." Ronnie said when he was gone.

"He's right. We fucked up." Nick said and walked out.

"I agree with Nick." Jason said and walked out leaving poor Ronnie by himself. To him this was not serious and he was only getting his friend's back last night like he had always been taught to do. He knew that if Bobby was there he would have done the same.

Before the meeting, Jack dropped Anna off at her apartment so that Bobby and Stacey could have alone time. When he picked her back up, he was almost in tears. He had just belittled his best friends, but he knew it wasn't going to be easy.

"How'd it go?" Anna asked getting in.

"I think I just lost three friends." He replied afflicted.

She rubbed the back of his head and said, "They're your friends and they love you. You didn't lose them; you just made them respect you more."

He smiled at her weakly and she pulled him in for a kiss. "You're sweet to say that, but I don't think it's true." He replied pulling the Maxima away from the curb. "They'll be at the meeting tonight so you can tell me what their body languages say."

"You know I can't read bodies! You should ask Bobby."
She replied.

"I will."

*"Why are there so many people here?" Bobby asked
Jason as they walked to the parking lot.*

*"I think there's a basketball tournament going on." He
replied pointing to the courts.*

*"Oh yea," Bobby said feeling dumb. He looked over and
could have sworn he saw Jackie G smiling at him from the
crowd, but it couldn't be. He broke off from Jason and
headed in pushing and shoving people out of his way.*

*He tripped over something and fell down. He looked up
and it was John holding Nick, who was on his knees, by his
hair.*

*"The Nation will fall." John said laughing like a crazed
person. He produced a shiny object, but before Bobby
realized what it was, the knife was in Nick's neck and blood
was spraying all over Bobby.*

*He got up gagging and spitting blood everywhere and
just like that John was gone. Nick was lying in a pool of his
own blood. Bobby tried to yell for help, but it was like no
one noticed what had just happened and the crowd closed
back up.*

*Bobby stood looking for Jason, but couldn't see him
anywhere. He spun around so fast that it made him dizzy.
When he stopped, he was met with Chris's smiling face.
Before Bobby could utter a word his face was shattered by
a huge fist, a fist bigger than he had ever seen.*

He fell to the ground and started tossing and turning.
"It's ok Bobby." A beautiful voice, as serene as an angel,
said. But at first it was distant, and then he heard it again,
"Its ok Bobby." This time it was closer. He thought he was
dead and this angel was coming to bring him for judgment,
but all at once everything started to fade and,

He woke up tossing and turning, Stacey was trying to settle him down. "It's ok Bobby." She said running her hand over his sweaty head and he realized it was just a dream. It didn't feel like a dream, he thought sitting up and looking around confused. "I'm here baby," Stacey said hugging his head against her chest. Instead of pushing her away he embraced her hold and it felt good.

"It was so real." Was the only thing he could think of saying.

"I heard." She replied. "You kept screaming and then you started yelling for Jason."

"Sorry," He said simply.

"It's ok; you don't need to be sorry." She pushed him away, then kissed his head and he could see tears in her eyes.

Just then the front door opened and Jack's voice filled the silent apartment. "Could you go keep them company while I get ready?" Bobby asked not wanting Jack to see him at that moment.

"Yea, sure, but Bobby," She paused then said, "No, nevermind."

"What is it?" He insisted.

"Bobby, you were sobbing like a baby." She said then turned and walked out.

"Thanks." He said, but she didn't hear him. He wiped at his eyes and they were wet.

He got dressed and walked out into the living room. Jack's face looked like a mixture of excitement and sadness.

"What's going on?" Bobby asked as he pulled on a t-shirt.

"I took care of everything." He replied despairingly.

"So then what's wrong?" Bobby asked carefully, seeing that Jack was on the verge of tears.

"They hate me, man. This shit is getting out of control." He blurted out. "I'm not sure if I can take it anymore." Bobby nodded towards Anna and Stacey. "No, its ok they can listen. They're as much a part of this as you or I." He finished dropping heavily onto Bobby's couch.

He told Bobby the plan he and Anna came up with, and then told him about the meeting he had at his house.

"Let's just get through tonight, then if you still feel the same way I'll take over as major and you can be my right hand man." Bobby said sitting next to him.

"Yea, I guess that would be ok. I think I need a drink, Bobby," But before he could finish Bobby backhanded him. "What the fuck was that for?" He almost screamed.

"If you drink it will be for fun, not because you're stressed." He replied.

Jack looked towards Anna for support, but she turned her head away saying, "He's right Jack."

"Did you think it was a fucking accident that she slept here last night?" Bobby yelled in his face. "Wake the fuck up! You scared her tough guy!"

Jack just put his head in his hands and said, "I'm sorry."

"Don't apologize, just cut the fucking shit." Bobby said coldly and got up.

"Where are you going?" Jack asked.

"For a run, so if you want a ride home come if not stay here." He said over his shoulder.

"Is it ok if I come?" Stacey asked quietly. She was trying not to piss off Bobby anymore.

"I promised you that you could, but if you can't keep up then don't blame it on me." He said giving her a sly smile and a wink that only she saw.

"Yea, we'll take the ride." Jack said ashamed.

"Ok well let's go!" Bobby exclaimed.

"When life is tough and you think you've messed up beyond repair, then that only means you're ahead of everyone else. Just fall back into the crowd until it's your time to break out again." Anna said kissing his forehead.

"I don't mean to sound rude, sweetheart, but what does that even mean?" Jack asked. He was about to cry, but years of training had taught him to hold it back.

"It was something my mom always used to tell me." She said shyly, "It basically means if you fuck up just relax. Go underground until people have forgotten then come back out of hiding."

"I don't know if I can do that, Bobby would kill me."

She chuckled a little. "In essence, it means that just because you fucked up, doesn't mean people don't love you anymore. Just relax and everything will blow over."

"I'm lucky to have you." He said kissing her throat.

"Jack, there is something I have to tell you before we continue our relationship." She said debating whether or not she should tell him.

"What is it?" He asked indifferently.

"I'm rich. Me and my sister have trust funds." She said biting her lower lip.

"What do you want a fucking cookie?" Jack asked just as indifferently. He looked up and tears started to form in her eyes and he said, "I didn't mean it like that."

"No, it's just that we're lucky to have you and Bobby." She said interrupting him.

"What do you mean?"

"Well, the reason my dad was so overprotective about us dating was because he thought guys would only be interested in our money," She put her head on his chest then whispered, "I can't wait for you to meet him."

"Me either," Jack said holding her, but thinking different, knowing how he felt about girl's parents.

To Bobby's surprise, Stacey not only kept up she was beating him. He was straining himself to keep up with her and she looked like she wasn't putting any effort in at all.

When they got to the tower across from the Meadow Glen mall Bobby took a pretend spill onto the grass. It wasn't that his sides hurt from getting jumped; in fact, he felt that they healed completely. It was the fact that he was out of shape that was killing him.

Stacey turned around and started jogging back to him. "I thought I was the one who wouldn't keep up." She said triumphantly.

"Oh I think I broke a rib." Bobby said holding his side and rolling back and forth.

"Oh my God, really," She asked putting her hands to her face.

"Yes!" He nearly screamed. She walked over to feel his sides and he grabbed her and rolled on top of her. "Gotcha, God I shoulda been an actor." He said tickling her sides.

"Bobby!" She screamed in between hysterical giggle fits.

It wasn't nice out by any means. There was frost on the ground, even, but that didn't stop Stacey from grabbing him by the shirt and pulling him down for a kiss.

"I'm going to kill you Bobby Cross." She said trying to sound like she was from the south and failing miserably at it.

"If you keep up with those accents, I just might die from laughing." He said smiling.

"Fuck you!" She exclaimed pushing him up.

"Right now, I'm into spur of the moment type of shit, but babe! We might get caught." He said.

"You're an asshole." She said trying to fight him off, but he was too heavy for her.

He leaned in to kiss her then pulled the hooded sweatshirt over her face and she roared with middle school girl giggles. He jumped up and started to run away, but Stacey was right on his heels and he let her tackle him to the ground.

"Bobby," She whispered looking deeply into his eyes.

"Yes?" He asked feeling better than he could ever remember.

"Tell me why you never trust women."

Bobby sighed and looked past her and into the bright sun. He knew it would come eventually, but he never really prepared to actually tell her. "My mom passed when I was four. I barely remember her, other than the fact that she was always there no matter how bad or good I was." He smiled at the memories, "She had cancer and the doctors found it a little too late. My father was a mess, I mean, he tried to raise me as best he could, but it was tough. He tried to go on several dates and they were all failed attempts at what he thought was love. Finally he met this girl who seemed perfect to him, I must have been eight at the time, and he married her.

"He didn't sign a prenuptial agreement even though everyone told him to. Now he wasn't rich, but he had a lot of money stashed away and when they divorced three years later she took everything. We went from living in a single family house over in Winchester to living in the Mystic Projects." He paused and gave her a weak smile, "He lasted one year there until he started drinking heavily and I had to take care of us. I was eleven, then four years later, I went to school one day and he decided to blow his head off with a twelve gauge. I found him after football practice. That bitch destroyed him. He was dead and Jack's parents took me in so I could finish off school in Somerville."

"I would never do that to you Bobby." She said not knowing what else to say.

"The funny thing is, is if Jack hadn't begged his parents, I don't know where I would be right now. They didn't want to take me in, because I was a trouble maker and everything, but," He smiled weakly and shrugged, "now you know why I don't trust women and why I love Jack so much. What he did for me is something I could never repay him for."

She started kissing him and only God knows how long they stayed there. Bobby felt good, at that moment in time nothing mattered. The Nation, Jack and even the dream he had was all forgotten at that moment in time. It was a good day, *was.*

14

On the way to Razzy's, Stacey looked over at Bobby and asked, "What was happening to Jason in your dream?"

He gave a crooked smile and said, "Nothing" As he grabbed her hand to hold.

"Don't lie to me Bobby, it was just a dream."

He sighed, looked over at her at a red light and said, "Nick got his throat cut and I was looking for Jason, but that didn't feel like no dream. It felt more real than right now does, if that makes any sense at all." Saying this out loud just made him feel stupid.

As he pulled into the parking lot at Conway, he seen everyone sitting around Ronnie's van, waiting for him he assumed. He pulled into the spot next to Ronnie's van and got out.

"What's going on guys?" He asked to no one in general.

"Nothing, we were just waiting for you." Jack said.

"Well, I'm here let's get in there." Bobby replied.

"No, we're going to do it out here. For some reason Razzy's is over packed tonight." Jack replied sounding confused. It was a Sunday night and it shouldn't be more packed than it normally is on a Saturday. "Hey ladies could you meet us in there?" Jack asked Lisa, Anna, Stacey and Kerry.

"Ok, well let's huddle around then, it should only take a second." Bobby announced aloud after the girls left. They all formed a circle around Jack and he instantly became nervous for some reason. "Jack let's go." Bobby said breaking his trance.

"Ok, sorry. Listen, guys, from now on you will be answering to Ronnie, Nick or Jason. They will in turn answer to Bobby who will then report to me."

"Sort of like the military?" Sam asked proudly.

"Yea, sort of," Jack answered then turned to where Nick was standing. "Two guys to each man, Ricky and Matt, you report to Nick. Sam and Sean, you report to Jason, Stubbs and Big Mike, you report to Ronnie." Everyone laughed at the last pair. "Alright, alright, settle down. This is only for business related purposes though." He looked around to make sure he had everyone's attention. "Last night, for example," He shouted, "will never, ever happen again. If you have a problem, then bring it up with Nick, Ronnie or Jason. If Nick, Ronnie or Jason has a problem then they will bring it up with Bobby." He stopped.

Bobby saw his hesitation and against his better judgment spoke up. "Listen, guys, we understand that last night was, for the most part, unavoidable, but next time walk away. We will regroup and then attack. Last night was not a fight for our Nation or even for our bar, but a petty drunken brawl over a girl and now we are in the headlines and on the cops' radars, especially you Nick. Your pretty face is all over Mass, probably even New England by now, even though it is fucked up. Not to mention someone is dead now."

When no one uttered a word Jack said, "Ok, let's go get drunk since there's no fight tonight." He paused and looked at Bobby, "For fun."

"Shouldn't we be worried about retaliation?" Big Mike asked then said, "Or should I ask Ronnie, I'm not being sarcastic."

"No, we should be ok, but watch out for anything unusual." Jack said smiling.

They all walked towards Razzy's like a mob. When they got to the front door there was a bouncer, who didn't even look like he was out of college.

"Whoa guys, we're at max capacity tonight." He said holding up his hands.

"Check again." Bobby said giving the kid the meanest look he could muster up without laughing.

"Come on I don't want any trouble." The Bouncer said.

"Are you fucking deaf? I told you to look again." Bobby growled this time and his voice was barely above a whisper.

"I did." The kid replied trying to sound tough. He even puffed out his chest and everything.

"Leave him alone Bobby. They're ok Shane." Nancy called from the doorway as Bobby cocked his fist back, but he was only going to threaten him.

"Ok, auntie." The kid said and let them pass.

"Auntie," Bobby asked.

"Yea, that's my nephew. He is qualified though." Nancy replied. "I have to warn you guys it is packed, but I could never deny you entrance."

"Why is it so packed?" Nick asked.

"I don't know. We got the karaoke machine up and working." She said walking back inside. Jack and Bobby just exchanged confused glances and followed her in.

It was an absolute mad house in there. Bobby thought to himself how this place was definitely more packed than he had ever seen and he has been going here since they first opened. He tried to scan the people and thought he saw some familiar faces, but there were just way too many people to be sure of that.

He nodded at Ruth and followed Jack to the back room. He thought he saw Chris from BSB, but he thought it was his mind playing tricks on him. He shook his head not knowing that Jack had the same exact thoughts not two feet in front of him.

They got to the bar in the back room, barely, and found Anna and Stacey sitting there with Lisa and Kerry. Two muscle bound guys were hitting on them, so Bobby walked up to them and said, "Get lost, now." Both guys turned as if to start trouble, but recognized Bobby and the rest of The Nation. They immediately obeyed Bobby and tried to fight through The Nation catching elbows and feet on the way.

"My knight in shining armor," Stacey said clasping her hands together and smiling brightly.

"Were they here long?" Bobby asked.

"Only since we sat down, God, it's like every guy thinks he'll get lucky if he gets a girl drunk enough." She said shaking her head.

"Darling, I don't mean to startle you, but does something seem a tic off?" He asked her in his best English accent.

"I don't know, but I have felt odd since I stepped in here. I can't put my finger on it and I think I saw that guy Chris you were talking to last night somewhere around here, but that can't be right I mean can it?" She asked.

"I thought I saw him too." He said scanning his surroundings starting to feel nervous.

"Bobby, um I not sure, but I think we're being set up." Jack said as the fire alarm went off. Talk about total chaos, everyone started running around in complete pandemonium. Jack and Bobby looked at each and knew at once that it was definitely a set up.

"Sam!" Jack called, but he couldn't hear through the confusion. He tried to grab him, but everyone kept running in between them. Before he knew it Sam was gone.

Bobby grabbed Jack by the shoulder and he took a swing at him in his nervousness, but Bobby was fast and ducked it easily.

"Take the girls and get the fuck out of here!" Bobby screamed in his face, trying to snap him out of whatever daze he was in. It wasn't working so Bobby turned around and grabbed a beer that was still almost full and splashed it in his face, this time it worked. "Take my car and get the fucking girls out of here!" He repeated.

"Shit, what if they get us on the way out?" He asked nervously.

"I'll make sure you get to the car just leave!" He yelled shoving Jack and then the girls so they formed a single file line.

Bobby didn't know what went through people's heads when they are in an emergency sort of situation, but nobody in Razzy's that night thought of going through the emergency exit door next to the stage.

Bobby yelled, "Back exit Jack!" He didn't have to, because that's where Jack was heading either way.

Jack kicked open the side door and ran down the alley and for some reason no one followed them. Jack kicked open the gate that led to the street and they stopped dead in their tracks. It looked like Times Sq during New Years Eve when the ball drops. People lined the sidewalk, on both sides, as far as the eye could see, and the street in between. There was easily double the amount of people Bobby had originally figured.

Bobby turned back to push them on, but they were no longer there. He spun around nervous as hell, spinning and spinning but saw no one. He heard the sirens, but saw no cops or ambulance. The only thing he could see was his breath and random faces. He fought his way through the crowd screaming out Nick's name, but there were too many people and too much confusion. He could only think of his dream at this point and he started to feel nervous again.

Somebody pushed him from the back sending him sprawling on the street. He spun around onto his ass and saw Chris standing over him with his arms crossed and a stupid grin on his face. He jumped up to his feet and went after Chris, but Chris backed into the crowd disappearing into the chaos. Bobby wanted to scream, but no one would hear him and so he pushed into the crowd to search for Chris.

Jack had just gotten into the parking lot when he started to hear the noise. He had no idea what it was, it kind of sounded like a knife on,

A guy from BSB, Jack recognized as Vinnie, was sitting on the curb rubbing his knife across the ground in a sharpening motion.

"Take that road all the way around." He said grabbing Anna by the shoulders and nodding towards a back entrance of Conway. "There won't be people that far down and if there are, run them over. Just get the fuck out of here."

"Come with me Jack, please." She said starting to cry.

He smiled at her and wiped a tear from her cheek. "I'll call you when this is over. Now get the fuck out of here!" He screamed and Vinnie's head rose. Jack kissed her on the lips and turned to Lisa, Stacey and Kerry, "If she can't drive then one of you do it." Stacey wasn't paying attention so he grabbed her hand gently and said, "He'll be fine."

"Why didn't he follow us?" She asked turning her head back towards him with the light shining off of her tears.

"I don't know, but I'm going to get him right now and then we'll meet back at my house. Now go!" He yelled again as he saw Vinnie getting on his cell phone.

He watched the girls go towards the Maxima and ran at Vinnie, who was trying to see what car they got into, not seeing Jack, and he kicked the phone out of Vinnie's hand, and then punched him in the face. Vinnie's nose exploded on impact and he fell on his back. Jack took the knife and threw it in one of the trash barrels, then came back to kick Vinnie in the head two more times for good measure.

He looked up and watched Lisa drive away with Anna and a sense of loss hit him hard almost knocking him down. He turned and ran back towards the crowd when they were out of sight behind the hockey rink.

The rest of The Nation had stuck together and were standing in front of Woody's Liquors across the street. Bobby had finally broken through the crowd and spotted big Mike leaning against a pole with the bus stop sign on it.

"Where's Nick?" He asked, yelling over the crowd, which was now getting out of control.

"He's taking a head count." He replied nodding back towards the rest of the group.

"Thanks." He said walking towards Nick. He grabbed Nick's shoulder and asked, "Is everyone here?"

"Yea, everyone's here except for you, Jack, Sam and Ronnie." He said scratching his head.

"Where the fuck is Sam and Ronnie?" Bobby asked

"I swear they were with us and then they just disappeared."

"Ok, everyone come hear!" He yelled and they formed a circle around him. "Listen, I know for a fact the BSB is here. I want everyone to spread out and look for Ronnie and

Sam. Keep your eyes open and your head on a God damned swivel. Rick and Matt will go with Nick, Jason you take Stubbs and Sean. Mike you're with me. We will meet back at Ronnie's van in fifteen. Nick, circle in from the right, Jason you go left and me and Mike will take the middle. Jack took the girls home so don't worry about him."

Bobby and Mike walked to the entrance of the parking lot and went into the crowd. He was pushing people out of the way and Mike was holding the back of his shirt so he didn't lose him. He started calling out Ronnie's name when he heard a girl scream.

Mike let go of Bobby's shirt and started in for the sound throwing people out of the way while Bobby came in like a running back following his lead blocker.

When they got to where they heard the sound, there was a little opening from where the crowd backed up, making room for the fight going on. Bobby came out and stopped dead in his tracks and all he could think of, was if this was really the dream he had and not reality.

Jack saw Bobby and Mike head into the crowd and ran in after. He lost them almost immediately, but found them again when the girl screamed. Instead of going to Bobby he also ran towards the scream.

By now the crowd was so loud that people couldn't hear the policeman on the loud speaker asking everyone to separate so the fire trucks could get in, so imagine how loud this girl's scream was, although only a twenty foot radius could hear her.

He emerged from the crowd to find Ronnie on his knees with Chris holding him by his hair. John was punching him in the face. Ronnie was just laying there limp and defenseless. Jack was so stunned that he found that he could not move from where he was standing for some reason.

Out of the corner of his eye he saw Mike running at them, but it was all in slow motion to him. His paralysis broke when he saw a guy tackle Mike. *So this is it huh, the endgame, the battle of battles.* He thought to himself as he sprinted in.

He caught someone trying to dive tackle him in his peripherals so he jumped in the air towards Chris. He hurdled over the guy and superman punched Chris all in one swift motion. He quickly spun around and saw Bobby head butt John to the ground, then landing on top of him. They were surrounded by BSB on all sides, but Bobby was just so fast that they had no chance to stop the head butt, but once he landed on top of him, he was immediately ripped off of John.

Chris was up and had his arm around Jack's throat choking him. He watched defenselessly as one guy had Bobby pinned, while another guy started punching him in the ribs. You couldn't even see Mike through all of the guys who were kicking him.

Jack was on the verge of blacking out and all he could think of was how he hoped that the girls made it home safely.

Some people in the crowd yelled, "Let's go Jack!", while others were yelling, "Get them Bobby!" He saw through blurred vision some people trying to help Mike, but there were just not enough of them.

All of a sudden the grip loosened around his throat and he fell to his knees. His vision came back clearer and clearer as he let out one violent whopping cough after another. When all vision was back he turned around slowly to see Sam with his finger in Chris's cheek, but Chris spun around fast with an elbow to his temple and Sam went down.

Jack acted immediately and tackled Chris to the cold cement street. Jack tried to throw shots, but Chris's hands went instinctively to his face to block them. He got maybe two punches in before he was ripped off. It was impossible to get an upper hand because they were coming out of the crowd from all sides.

Chris sat up, but Sam was back on top, trying to fishhook him again. Jack loved the heart in this kid and that was the last thought he had before his world went gray and then black.

Bobby saw Jack get hit in the head with a slapjack and go down like a sack of potatoes. Acting purely on adrenaline, he leaned back, brought his feet up and when the guy tried to get closer, Bobby kicked out as hard as he could connecting with the guy's face and knocking him out cold. He threw his head back connecting with the other guy's nose. It made a sickly cracking sound and Bobby knew he broke the nose. He spun around with his elbow and connected with the nose again, causing the kid to scream in pain.

The guy who hit Jack was now walking towards Sam, who still had the fishhook in Chris's mouth. Bobby grabbed the guy's hair and pulled him down from behind. The guy flew in the air in comedic style and landed with a thud and a loud grunt as he lost the air in his lungs. He lifted his head, trying to get a better breath, but Bobby kicked him in the face and his head bounced off of the ground like a basketball. His eyes rolled to the back of his head and Bobby said, "Night, night bitch."

Bobby looked over at Sam as he ripped Chris's cheek apart and it started spraying blood out. Chris moaned and rolled over holding his wound. Sam then started punching him on the other cheek.

Bobby grabbed him up, screamed "Mike," in his face and pointed to the crowd of people hovering over what he thought would be big Mike. They ran over and started knocking people off of him. They finally got to Mike, who was still conscious, but bloody and badly hurt.

Bobby helped him up and he stumbled a little bit then caught his balance and roared with anger. He grabbed one guy and lifted him in the air with one hand by the throat.

Bobby ran over to Ronnie, who wasn't moving. Bobby put his finger under his nose to see if he was still breathing. He was, but it was weak. He smacked him lightly a couple of times, but nothing happened, he didn't move an inch.

He heard Jack groaning and ran over to him. "You alright boss?" He asked nervously.

"Oh man I feel like I'm gonna," He started then puked all over the ground. Steam rose off of it and he looked at Bobby, "Now I feel better."

"Ok get out of here, now." Bobby replied.

"No way, this shit's personal." He said trying to stand, but fell back to his knees.

"Dude just go, it's over! Mike and Sam are finishing up with them." He said waving his hand towards them. Mike still had the one guy in the air trying to take the life right out of him.

"Ok, I'll go call Anna to come pick me up." He replied trying to get up again. He fell, but Bobby caught him.

"Wait a second." Bobby said putting him back down and running over to Mike and Sam. "Guys, can you take Jack out of here so he can call Anna?"

Mike gave him a look, he didn't want to let the guy go, but when Bobby thought he was going to kill him, Mike just dropped the guy and jogged over to Jack with Sam close behind. The guy sat there grasping his throat and was gratefully taking every ounce of oxygen he could with each breath. Bobby helped him up to show good faith and the guy accepted willingly.

He walked back over to Ronnie who was still out cold. A group of people had since formed a protective circle around him and Bobby said, "I appreciate this more than you will ever know. Could you make sure no one hurts him anymore?"

"Of course," Some guy answered who looked very familiar to him.

"Thank you." He said then paused and stuck out his hand. "Sorry about pulling you off the bar like that."

"Hey I was acting like an," he started then his eyes widened, "Look out Bobby!"

Bobby spun and there were ten BSB members coming towards him. Most of them were new. "Who the fuck are you guys?" He yelled.

"Reinforcements," One guy answered with an evil grin.

"Fuck me then." He replied walking towards them to keep them away from Ronnie.

"Yes," the guy said laughing, "fuck you" and they formed a circle around him.

Bobby stood his ground and thought maybe they would come at him one at a time like in the movies, but all at once they came at him. Bobby took one guy out with a haymaker, but that was all.

The crowd started chanting, well not so much chanting as calling, "Nation! Nation! Nation!"

They would cheer, but not one of them would step in and help Bobby and Bobby could only think of how much life was a bitch.

Nick and Jason met back up in front of Razzy's. They had no idea about what had happened. "You see anyone?" Nick asked.

"No, but this shit's gonna get broken up real soon. You see how many cops are here?" Jason replied.

"Definitely be on the news later." Matt said with a hint of excitement in his voice.

"Yea, no doubt, I counted at least ten cruisers on my side and none of them were from Somerville." Jason said.

"Jesus, this is nuts." Nick said and then heard the chant start. "What the fuck is that?"

"I don't know, but it's coming from in there." Stubbs said pointing to the middle of the crowd.

"Well they're calling for us, so let's go!" Nick yelled as the chant started spreading throughout the crowd like wildfire.

Jason led the way like a bulldozer. Anyone who was in his was way got knocked over, he would do anything to get to the middle. When they finally emerged Bobby was in a boxing stance, but he was swaying. There were eleven guys now, John had gotten up and the kid Mike choked got in the mix, even though Bobby had helped him up.

At first no one moved and then Jason started running and the rest followed suit. They had the upper hand as the BSB's back was to them. They all took one guy each leaving five guys jumping Bobby.

Stubbs punched the biggest guy in the back and the guy just slowly turned around as if the punch hadn't affected him at all. Stubbs had to jump in the air to reach his face. The guy kept dodging the punches toying with him. Stubbs got frustrated and punched him in the balls as hard as he could, which brought the guy to his knees clutching his nuts. Then Stubbs jumped on top of him and brought head butts and elbows down on the defenseless man's face.

Matt grabbed one guy's hair from the back and kicked his legs out. He just stomped on his face, not too hard, but hard enough to knock him out.

Jason kicked one guy in the back making him sprawl forward. He got up and spun around. He tackled Jason, but on the way down Jason lifted his knee and knocked the guy out. The guy fell on top of him and started snoring. This guy was at least two times heavier than Jason was, so he couldn't move him.

Rick bulldogged one guy into the ground. He turned the guy over and thought he killed him until he spit out teeth and blood. He got up and kind of tip toed away and ran out through the crowd.

Sean jumped in front of his guy and threw his elbow back as hard as he could and the guy fell like a tree. He turned to make sure he didn't get back up, but there was no way this guy would be getting up anytime soon.

Nick shoved the back of the guy's head, not hard, but enough to make him stumble forward a step or two. He whirled around with disturbing speed and took a boxer's stance against Nick. Nick came forward with a quick combo, but the guy blocked all the punches then threw a kick at Nick's shin for good measure. Obviously he was an experienced fighter, so Nick couldn't take him lightly. He got into his stance and went in. The guy kicked him in the ankle, ribs and side of the head so fast that Nick was confused about what the hell had just happened. He took a step back to weigh out his options and the guy started showing off his karate skills. Nick smiled to himself and waited for the opportune moment to strike. The guy finished with a back flip and Nick went in timing it just right so that when he landed Nick's fist met with his face.

Nick looked down and said, "Fucking moron, who does that?" but the guy was out cold and would not hear him.

Bobby was still standing, but barely. Once the other guys realized what was going on they turned to fight. All except for John, who was now squaring up with Bobby. Blood mixed with sweat dripped down his forehead and stung his eyes. Bobby wiped it out and stood straight. The only thing keeping him up was pride and maybe the thought of getting back to Stacey.

The chant went from "Nation" to "FCN" and it was the whole entire crowd now. Bobby even saw a couple of cops cheering them on. He spit out blood and looked at John, who was looking at him. Steam was rising off of both of their heads. He took a deep breath and went in.

Jack circled back around the crowd and went in trying to lose Sam and Mike, now that he had his balance. He heard the chant and immediately knew something was wrong. He saw his opening and said, "Oh man," and started for the gap.

"Where are you going Jack?" Mike asked and Jack just pointed and went in.

Right when he got in he started zigzagging through people staying as low as possible. There was no possible way for Mike and Sam to keep up, but they tried all the same.

He came out in the clearing and just saw bodies everywhere. It reminded him of a war movie with all the casualties lying everywhere. He seen Jason struggling with the fat guy on top of him and went over to help. He rolled him off and held out his hand.

"How's it going?" Jack asked when Jason was on his feet.

"Except for that lard ass falling on me? Fucking great, where's Ronnie?" He asked not knowing what happened.

"Last time I saw him he was on the ground over there." Jack replied pointing to the crowd of yuppies standing in a circle.

They turned as one guy took a swing at Jason and connected good sending him back down. Jack punched him in the throat and walked away not looking back. He had to check on Ronnie.

Sam and Mike Came out a few minutes later and saw the guy gasping for air and grabbing his throat. Sam punched him in the face and Mike went to check on Jason.

Chris came out of nowhere and tackled Sam to the ground. His cheek was flapping and blood was still pouring out onto Sam's face. Chris was putting his finger into Sam's cheek when Mike lifted him off of Sam and threw him like a ragdoll. He came up on top of him quickly after, and then started punching him, but not wanting to hurt him only wanting to stop him. He achieved that when Chris was limp.

The rest of BSB was disposed of easily now that they were outnumbered. Only one stood and he was looking at Bobby, both of them looking like two boxers who went the distance. Nick stepped up to jump in, but Jack put his hand out to stop him. Nick looked at him and Jack just shook his head. Nick shrugged and went to Ronnie.

To the crowd outside of the circle, people were chanting to be assholes, but to the people who could see, well they were chanting for two warriors who refused to give up.

The cops started tossing tear gas into the crowd, but not close enough to these people who were enjoying the free show. Sure, it would all be broken up in a few minutes, but as far as any of them were concerned they had all the time in the world.

Bobby stumbled like a drunken person as he tried to swing and missed. John swung and hit Bobby's shoulder. He shrugged it off and grabbed John's T-shirt and pulled him in. John fell into Bobby's punch more than Bobby actually connected and for some reason it made John regain some balance. He grabbed Bobby's shirt and they just punched each other. No one blocked or dodged, they just connected with each others face, one bone rattling punch after the other. It was a pure old fashioned hockey fight. I'm not talking about short jabs or sloppy haymakers; these were pinpoint, accurate and hard. The longer they punched, the faster they got. There was no one clearly winning the fight and it looked like they were holding each other up which is why Stubbs came up to Jack and said, "We have to stop it now."

"Let it go until someone falls." Jack said trusting his cousin and knowing that if he did try to stop it he was liable to get attacked by both men, not to mention Bobby feeling disgraceful after. It was something Jack would not do.

Bobby connected and knocked John back a couple feet. He came back at Bobby swinging and missing. Bobby grabbed his shirt again and pulled him in and they went back and forth like a rockem sockem robots battle, punching each other until someone's head pops off.

John finally went down and Bobby stumbled towards Jack who caught him. The crowd went silent.

Bobby pushed off of Jack, staggered a little bit and once he was sure he had his balance he raised his head. It was covered in blood. He smiled a sickly smile, his teeth were stained red with blood, and then he looked to the sky and started yelling for no reason he knew of. He raised his arms, but not in victory or defeat, but just to do it. It could have been because he saw it in a movie or could have been because he was alive and he felt it was the right thing to do, either way, he felt liberated.

He looked at Jack and let out a groaned chuckle then collapsed to his knees in exhaustion. Someone in a suit ran over before Jack could move and knelt next to him with a badge and gun hanging off of his belt and asked, "Are you ok son?"

He nodded and said, "Ronnie, my friend."

"Who," The man asked.

"Ronnie." Bobby said trying to get up.

"Easy now," The cop said and helped him up.

He allowed Bobby to lead him to where the yuppies were still obediently guarding Ronnie. They parted for Bobby and he pointed to Ronnie and fell to his knees again.

The guy produced a cell phone and dialed a number. He yelled into it, "I need a paramedic in the middle of this circle right now!" Then he checked Ronnie's vitals. "He's still breathing, but his pulse is weak."

"Is that good or bad?" Jack asked from behind.

"I don't know yet, we need to get him to the doctor, but you guys need to leave right now. Bobby, do you need to see a doctor do you think?" He asked.

"No," He paused wiping his eyes and said, "Thank you, detective Morales."

"Ok, buddy, get out of here though. More cops will be here any minute."

Bobby got up to leave and pulled out a cigarette which that yuppie lit for him and then handed him a zip up hooded sweatshirt. "Your shirt is ripped, this could help," He said.

Bobby thanked them again then turned to Seth and asked, "When you find out what hospital he's at will you call me?"

There were only five layers of people now, after the fight was over tear gas was getting thrown closer to the center, causing the crowd to disperse faster than before. The paramedics were breaking through these people now and Seth said, "Yes now leave before you get caught, I'll make sure they don't trace him."

Bobby put his arm around Jack for support and they walked to the van, where everyone already was waiting per Jack's orders. Jack looked in the gas tank and the keys were there, like always.

He looked out at everyone and said, "Whoever needs a ride home, get in the van. The rest of you, go home. Tonight is over and done with. I'll call everyone in the morning."

15

"Why haven't they called?" Stacey asked pacing back in forth in between Jack's bedroom and kitchen.

"I don't know." Anna replied with tears streaming down her face.

When they were pulling out of the parking spot they saw the man scraping the knife against the cement and then they saw Jack go after him, but that was all. She didn't know if he'd been stabbed. She didn't know if he was in a hospital ER or in the morgue somewhere. She couldn't do anything except sit on Jack's bed holding his football t-shirt to her nose, smelling his scent and longing to be in his arms once more.

"He'll be fine." Lisa said then looked at Stacey. "They'll both be fine." Then thought again and knew Kerry had been crushing on Ronnie and said, "They'll all be fine."

Stacey gave her a weak smile. She didn't want to tell her that this was all her fault. She had to flirt with that guy from the BSB and put Bobby in danger. She was a good friend and meant well. So she just said, "Thank you, but I know something's wrong. It's just been too long."

The door opened and Jack stepped in with Bobby, who was a bloody mess, still helping him walk. He looked up and saw tears start streaming down Stacy's cheeks. He gave her a smile and said, "Hey there beautiful, miss me?"

"Who is that?" Anna called from Jack's room. Jack stepped in the doorway and Anna freaked out. She got up and jumped on him wrapping her legs around his waist and started kissing him on the mouth. Jack was still weak from the beating he took and collapsed under her weight. She landed on top of him, but didn't care when he grunted or if he was in pain, she was in his arms once again and that was all that mattered to her.

Stacey was gently canvassing Bobby's fucked up face. It was swollen like a balloon. There were several deep gashes in his forehead and the cut he had from before on his brow had reopened. He had a broken nose and his lip was split in two different places.

"You need to go to the hospital Bobby." She whispered through sniffles.

"You can be my nurse." He replied wiping a tear from each eye with blood crusted thumbs. She didn't mind, though, just feeling his touch again made her happy.

"No, Bobby, you need stitches. That's why you have so much blood on your face right now." She said pointing to the gashes.

"I'll live." He replied. "Jack can I use one of your towels?" He called into the room, but got no reply so he just took one and used it to wipe the blood off.

"Where is everyone else?" Stacey asked.

"We dropped everyone off, but Jason stayed behind to see if he could get any information."

He wiped away the blood, but most of it was dried already and fresh blood poured through the gash.

"Gimme it," Stacey said and took the towel. She damped it with warm water and cleaned his face off as gently as she could, trying not to hurt him.

She made Lisa stop at their apartment in Cambridge after they left Conway so she could grab her supplies just in case. She opened her medical bag and put ten butterfly stitches across his forehead then wrapped gauze around the top of his head and finished by wrapping an ace bandage over that. She stepped back and examined her work and said, "That won't hold too long, how are your ribs?"

"Oh, they hit me there a lot." He said putting his hand there.

"You didn't wrap it did you?" She asked sounding sad.

He lifted up his shirt and smiled. "I listen to some of the things you tell me to do."

She took out a pen light and said, "Brace yourself, this'll hurt."

"Ok," Bobby replied confused.

She put the pen light up one of her nostrils and put her hand against the other nostril. She quickly pushed on the nostril producing a cracking sound. Blood started coming out of his nose and his eyes started watering. She put a brace on the nose then kissed his cheek.

"See, no big deal," He said.

She smiled at him and said, "Bobby those are going to be some awful scars. You should really go to the doctor."

"I don't care as long as you don't leave me because I'm a freak." He replied then put his arms around her and pulled her into him and whispered, "Thank you."

"For what," She asked and Bobby could feel her tears roll down her cheek and onto his neck.

"You kept me alive tonight," He replied, "I thought it was pride, but the thought of you and getting to you for this very moment is what kept me standing. You are my new reason for living."

She pulled back and looked in his one eye that wasn't swollen shut. "What are you talking about?"

"I didn't quit because all I could see was you waiting for me." He replied and pulled her back into his embrace. She just allowed it not wondering about what had actually happened, not really caring. Bobby was alive and that was all that mattered.

Anna pulled her hand off the back of Jack's head and said, "Jack you're bleeding! What the fuck."

"Oh someone hit me in the back of the head, I'm fine." He said bringing his hand to the spot absent mindedly.

"You better have Stacey look at that." She said rising off of him.

"No sweetheart I'm fine." He replied looking up at her, wanting more of her touch.

She gave him a scolding look then ordered, "You get in there and have her check you out before I pop you one." She put her fist up threateningly.

"Pop me one?" He asked cracking up laughing.

"What? That was tough." She said smiling through her tears.

"I love you." He replied still laughing.

Kerry asked in a sad quiet voice. "Guys, what about Ronnie?"

Bobby and Jack gave each other a look before Bobby sighed. He let go of Stacey to put a hand on Kerry's shoulder and said, "He was beaten unconscious. He was still breathing and they took him to a hospital, I don't know which one, but they're gonna let me know, I'm sorry Kerry."

"Thank you Bobby." She replied then buried her head into Lisa's shoulder. She sobbed quietly for a long time.

"It doesn't look good guys." Jason said outside of Mass General.

They didn't want to go inside because of all the suspicion going around about them being in the fight and burning down Razzy's. Seth told cops that Ronnie was just a guy who got hit unexpectedly during the riot and Jason was his brother.

"He's in a coma right now and the doctor's say it don't look good. He's bleeding in the brain." Jason said somberly.

"So what the fuck does that mean?" Bobby asked.

"His brain is swollen and he could die." Jason replied.

Bobby started away and Jack grabbed him and asked, "Where are you going?"

"To say goodbye to one of my best friends," He replied and kept walking.

"Well then let's go." Jack replied then started after him. The Nation fell in line and followed their leader into the waiting room.

"Sir you can't go in there." A doctor said trying to stop him.

"Watch me." Bobby said and continued into Ronnie's room.

The doctor told the nurse to call security, but Nick and Sam took up guard in front of the door and wouldn't let anyone go in.

Security came up right away. They saw Sam and Nick then sighed. "Get out of the way, please."

"No." Sam said firmly.

"Are we going to have to call the cops?" One of them asked.

"You do what you need to do, but I guarantee he'll be done before they get here." Nick said.

"You can try to use force if you would like, but that wont help you too much." Sam said smiling.

The two guards knew of everyone in the waiting room, seen the news article on Bobby and read the paper containing Nick's face, so they kind of gave up and told the doctor that if he wanted them gone, he would have to call the cops, because there was no way they were going to fight a bunch of hooligans.

"I'm sorry man" Bobby said looking down at Ronnie. "I shouldn't have let you go off by yourself." He paused and

looked into Ronnie's lifeless face, "Dream well my friend."
He kissed his forehead and left.

As he left the hospital his phone rang, "How is he?" The
voice asked.

"How did you know?"

"I told you not to go there; they are looking to arrest
somebody, Bobby."

"Why didn't you arrest me that night, detective?"

"What I saw, was amazing," He started, "Two gladiators
that didn't understand the word quit. Do not get me
wrong Mr. Cross, I will arrest you next time something like
that happens, but that was the best fight I have ever seen
in my life. It would have been a shame to arrest you that
night."

"I appreciate everything you have done for me and the
Nation, especially Ronnie. I will not soon forget it." Bobby
replied and hung up.

16

Two months later Bobby was staring at the picture of Ronnie they decided to use, the one of him and the guys the first time they went to Razzy's, then he looked out at everyone gathered in the pews of the church. He looked at all the people who were gathered at the front of the church when the organ music started playing.

Bobby looked at Nick and Jason and asked, "Are you guys ready for this?" They both answered by nodding nervously. Bobby took a deep breath and put his hand on Jack's shoulder, "Can you handle this?"

Jack looked at Ronnie's picture then at his cousin. He had tears in his eyes, but was keeping himself under control and said, "I hope so."

"I'll be right here." Bobby said as Jack walked down the three steps to take his fiancée's hand from her father.

They walked back up to stand in front of the priest and Bobby stared across at Anna's maid of honor and smiled. Their lives had taken a drastic change, but for the first time in Bobby's life it was for the good.

Ronnie was still in a coma, but he was doing better. The doctor, Stacy and Annabelle's mother, told them that his brain activity was steadily increasing every day and it was only a matter of time until he woke up. They had his picture there because Jack didn't want one of his groomsman to miss the wedding, which they had already pushed back too long waiting for him.

John apologized on behalf of the BSB for over reacting and getting crazy that night. Jack accepted the apology saying that Chris's cousin dying plus getting fish hooked was punishment enough. Besides, John and Bobby's fight was one for the ages and people would write stories about it. The video on the internet was already over five million views. If Ronnie wasn't showing signs of improvement, it probably would have been a different story.

Razzy's never reopened after the fire. Whether it was because the damage was just too severe, or Nancy was sick of everything, Bobby would never know. One thing he did know was he would miss the hell out of that place. Last Bobby heard, Nancy had moved somewhere north to open a butcher shop, but he didn't know how true that was.

Bobby thought about that night often. He thought about how much Stacey outweighed his pride when it came to not giving up and wondered if this couldn't be the girl to get him to stop fighting. He knew he would never stop fighting, because after all, he'd been fighting his whole life. Not only physical fist fights, but fighting to keep himself alive when his father went to drinking and after his father died.

He took a haul of his cigarette and put his elbows on the railings overlooking the ocean. He turned around and looked in at the reception going on. He looked in at the table set up for the FCN and smiled. Stubbs was getting animated while telling a story. They were his new extension of brothers.

Jackie G called Bobby (he didn't have Jack's number) and asked why they cancelled the brawls for the Fighting Cox and Minutemen games. Bobby gave him a rundown about everything that had happened and Jackie understood. For a Minutemen fan he wasn't such a bad guy, he even gave Jack a wedding present, it was a Minutemen jersey, but who gives a shit, it's the thought that counts. He said he couldn't wait until next year to fight Bobby.

"Hey there good looking." Stacey said breaking him from his thoughts.

Bobby smiled and said, "Stop being nice, I look like a freak."

She walked up to him and kissed the scar on his brow and then the one on his forehead and said, "Nope, you're the most handsome man here." She put her arms around his waist and put her ear to his chest and said, "I'm happy for them."

"Me too," Bobby replied, "I haven't seen Jack this happy in a long time."

"Honey we want to take a family photo." Stacey's father called out from the doorway. "You come too Bobby, you're a part of this family now."

"Give me a couple of minute's sir, I'm feeling a little sick." Bobby replied.

The father's name was also Robert, but he didn't like any nicknames. Bobby liked him though, no nonsense and straight to the point. He had even told Bobby he would fight him if he had hurt his daughter. There is something admirable about a father who will go to any extremes to protect his daughter, even tell a man covered in scars he would fight him.

"Go on, babe," he said kissing the top of Stacey's head.

She went back in and Bobby turned to look out at the endless ocean.

"What's next?" Jack asked putting his elbows up next to Bobby's.

"Next, my friend, you go on your honeymoon and make me a nephew." Bobby replied clapping him on the shoulder.

"I'm talking about The Nation." Jack replied solemnly.

"Well let's see, you created a monster with this thing, but I'm behind you all the way, so whatever you decide."

"I don't know man."

"Well, how do you feel about the Canadians?" Bobby asked winking at him. "Take a little road trip and get some practice in."

"Nah," They said at the same time laughing.

"What if we start a family and I don't want to do this anymore?" Jack asked.

Bobby thought a second and took a final haul off of his cigarette then said, "Then you step down. If this takes off like I know it will, then you'll go down as the guy who started it all. You'd be a legend."

"What did we do wrong Bobby? Why didn't this go as smoothly as it did in Green Street Hooligans?"

"Well that was a movie and England has been doing this for years, since the beginning of soccer probably." He tossed his filter into the sea then squinted into the sun. "I think our problem was that we tried to organize it better, but in England I think they just do because of the love they have for their team, and we sort of lost sight of that passion. We tried to make it too Hollywood, sort of." He sighed and turned around

"Yea, I guess you're right."

"Honey let's go." Anna yelled to Jack.

"Husband duties," Jack said winking at Bobby and then went in.

Bobby thought about what was next. Maybe he'd take a trip to England to see how it was really done or he could buy Stacey a ring. He chuckled aloud at the idea, but was it really that crazy? She had moved in with him and he knew for a fact he loved her, so what was the big deal?

It was absolutely insane how much he matured over the course of the past couple of months and a lot of it could be contributed to Stacey. She showed him he belonged to something, something he never thought he'd ever have again, a family.

As if queued in by some greater power Stacy came out, "Robert Cross, get your ass in here and take this God damned picture so you can dance with me."

He smiled off into the vast ocean and turned, "On my way."

After the pictures Bobby went to the bar, to get away from dancing and Jack's father was standing there. Bobby knew that he wasn't exactly Jack's father's favorite person but was surprised when he asked, "What are you drinking Bobby?"

"I'll have a Jack and Coke,"

"Make that two," He said, "and two shots of Jamison."

"You think you can handle that, old man?" Bobby said with a grin.

"Boy, I would drink you under the table," He replied and put an arm around Bobby, "You think I don't know what's been going on."

"What do you mean?"

"I mean, I know about Jack's plan to start a gang."

"I," Bobby started.

"I know I haven't been the best uncle to you, but ever since my sister died," He paused, "I know she would be proud of the man standing before me today."

"Thank you," Bobby said taking a sip of his Jack and Coke feeling confused.

"I am glad my son has someone like you watching his back. You care more about him then you do yourself and that is a rare trait in a person, loyalty."

"He's my brother."

Jack's father smiled weakly and said, "And you are my son, I'm so sorry I haven't been there more." They clanked glasses and took the shot then he said, "You want to see something funny, let's go watch Jack try to dance."

They walked back to the reception and Stacey came out of nowhere and grabbed Bobby's hand and started to pull, "No, I'm talking to my uncle," Bobby protested.

"It's ok, son, we'll finish later," Jack's father said taking Bobby's Jack and Coke, laughing at him.

They got to the middle of the dance floor and Bobby had to thank God that a slow song came on. Stacey gritted her teeth and said, "You're very lucky mister," before putting her hands on his shoulders.

"Yes I am," Bobby replied and pulled her close and kissing her.

"I need to tell you something," She said pulling back.

"What?"

"I'm late,"

"It's only seven," He said looking at his watch.

"No, Bobby, I might be pregnant." She tried to measure his reaction, but his face was stone and she was getting nervous, "Bobby?"

He finally smiled and said, "That's the best news I've ever heard, I'll be a dad."

She smiled and said, "I love you."

CPSIA information can be obtained
at www.ICGtesting.com
Printed in the USA
BVHW041401180420
577887BV00009B/369

9 781477 582237